Th
r

A Chocolate Centered Cozy Mystery Series

Cindy Bell

ISBN-13: 978-1517065850

ISBN-10: 1517065852

Table of Contents

Chapter One

Screeching tires jolted Ally Sweet from the relaxed state she had settled into. A car swerved across the highway in front of hers. It corrected, and straightened out into the lane. A quick shake of her head cleared the panic caused by the near-collision.

"Peaches, you okay?" She looked over at the carrier buckled into the passenger seat beside her. After receiving a reassuring meow Ally focused on the traffic around her. It was a familiar drive, but over the years it had become much more congested. She was relieved when she finally passed the city limits sign.

Ally grew up an hour outside of the city, but her hometown was like another planet. She was just taking a short break, but her heart ached as she knew she was finally leaving behind not just a broken marriage, but also the life she had built. However, the draw of where she was headed kept her tears at bay. Going home triggered memories of heat billowing out of an oven door, or laughter filtering in from the back porch, of little fingers plucking at piano keys.

Ally longed for the presence of her grandmother in ways that she longed for little else. She seemed to make the world make sense, and if it didn't for some reason, she would put it back in place. Ally took the next exit off the highway. The sign boasted 'Mainbry', but the name of the small town where she was headed was Blue River. The town got its name from the glistening blue river running through it. After only a few miles the scenery changed from pavement and concrete to fields dotted with cows and a handful of farm houses. A whiff of manure, freshly cut grass, and the promise of rain, was the smell that greeted Ally. She was home.

She turned down the long, dirt driveway of her grandmother's property with a sense of completion bolstering her. Whenever she heard the crunch of the rough road beneath the tires of her car she knew that she was home. She only had one foot out of the car when the front door of the small cottage burst open.

"Ally! Ally! Oh she's here, Arnold!" A petite, gray-haired woman wearing a bright floral dress bounded down the steps of the front porch. On her lightly lipsticked mouth was the biggest grin that Ally had ever seen. She always thought her grandmother had a way of sharing how she was feeling without ever saying a word. Without hesitation she rushed forward to meet her grandmother at the bottom of the steps. Her initials were carved into one corner of the bottom step. A fond smile rose to her lips at the memory of etching them into the soft wood. She opened her arms to her grandmother as she had ever since she was a little girl. Arnold charged right up beside her.

"Hi Mee-Maw, hi Arnold." Ally's heart swelled with love at the sensation of her grandmother's arms wrapping around her. She didn't even mind that Arnold was sniffing at her pocket. Arnold was known around town for his good sniffer.

"Arnold, do be polite." Charlotte clucked her tongue with disapproval. Arnold scurried off into the house. For a rather portly pot-bellied pig he could actually move pretty fast.

"Let me look at you, honey." Charlotte swept her piercing gaze over Ally from the top of her head to the tips of her toes. Ally didn't feel criticized. Her grandmother had been looking her over this way since she was a young child. "My my, the city did good things for you."

"Did it?" Ally looked at her with a sullen frown. "Doesn't really feel that way."

"Well, you just need some sun on your cheeks and some chocolate in your belly." She laughed and waved Ally into the house. Ally followed after her. There was little in life that she loved more than spending time with her grandmother. Their relationship had blossomed from parent and child to a close friendship.

The inside of the cottage was just as she remembered it. There were soft reminders of the past everywhere in picture frames, needlepoint, and even old pictures that Ally had painted as a child. She shouldn't have been surprised as it hadn't been that long since she had been there last, but after everything that had happened over the past few months she felt as if it had been a century.

"Come, have some tea with me." Charlotte steered her into the kitchen. The kitchen held the most intense memories for Ally. She had spent hours as a young child sitting underneath the round kitchen table. She would play with her dolls, or imagine new worlds, while the grown-ups above her discussed all of the heavy things that life had dealt. Ally was under that table the day her mother admitted that Ally's father had simply walked away. Ally barely remembered the exact words, but she did remember the scent of vanilla and cinnamon, which her grandmother always put in her tea.

"Here you are." Charlotte set down Ally's favorite cup and saucer. It was a sky blue set with big yellow stars painted on the side. Ally's mother had made it when she was a child. Ally picked up the cup as she sat down.

"Thanks, Mee-Maw."

"I've missed you."

"I've missed you, too." Ally looked into her eyes. "More than you know."

"What's going on, my love?" Charlotte reached across the table and took Ally's free hand in her own. "Tell me all about it."

"I just wanted to come for a visit."

Peaches rubbed her long, orange body along Ally's leg. She felt the tickle of the cat's tail.

"I'm sure you did. But I'm sure there's a lot more to it than that. Hmm?" She arched a perfectly sculpted eyebrow. Ally always admired her grandmother's beauty. It was classic in the sense that it didn't require a lot of make-up. Her features were more strong than feminine, and her flowing, gray hair should have aged her. Instead, to Ally, it made her grandmother magical. The bold green eyes that gazed at her were the same that Ally saw in the mirror each day. They weren't just a similar shade, they were the same shape and color. When Ally looked into her grandmother's eyes, she found it very difficult to tell a lie. This little problem had made getting through high school challenging for her.

"All right, all right." Ally sighed and took a sip of her tea. As she set the saucer back down she rounded her shoulders forward. "I might not be handling the divorce as well as I first thought."

"Well, how does one handle something like that?" Charlotte's lips pursed briefly as if she was trying to hold back a tirade. This was fairly unusual for her, as Ally was used to her grandmother always saying what she thought. "I mean, it's not as if you changed dentists, we're talking about the breaking of vows."

"It wasn't like that, Mee-Maw. We just didn't get along anymore."

"Because he's a heartless, immature beast of a man who wants nothing more than a servant for a wife." Charlotte smacked the table lightly with her fingertips. "Does that about cover it?"

Ally tried not to smile. "Mee-Maw, there's two sides to every story. I was at fault, too. It just didn't work out."

"So, do you think he's sipping tea and thinking about it somewhere?"

Ally's cheeks flushed. She knew that he wasn't. In fact she was fairly certain that he was with a friend of hers, and not likely thinking about her at all.

"No, I guess not."

"See?" Charlotte shook her head. "Honey, I've always told you, you've got a big heart, and that's beautiful, but your brain has got to be bigger."

"Mee-maw!"

"I'm sorry. I'm just telling the truth." Charlotte blushed a little. "Was that too far?"

"I just thought it would get better. I mean, everyone kept telling me, just give it a few more years, it will get better." Ally took the last sip of her tea, with the hope that it would calm her nerves.

"I never told you that."

"You're right. You were the only one that didn't." Ally stared down at the table top. Her mind flooded with the memories of all of the conversations she and her grandmother had shared regarding her marriage. Not once did her grandmother advise her to wait it out. Instead she had pointed out that Ally had already given up so much of herself, and still he was not content. Ally's eyes moistened with tears.

"Hey now, beautiful." Charlotte caught Ally by the chin and tilted her head up so that she could meet her eyes. "You didn't do anything wrong. Love is love, and it will do as it pleases. Unfortunately, you are not the first woman in this family to marry the wrong man, and I feel certain you won't be the last."

"Is that supposed to make me feel better, Mee-Maw?" Ally offered a half-smile. She blinked back her tears.

"There's nothing I can say to make you feel better. That's entirely up to you." She gave Ally's chin a light pinch. "Don't you fret though. There are millions of men on this earth."

"Oh no, thank you, I gave it a go, I think I'll fly solo from now on." Ally stood up to clear away the tea cups from the table.

"We'll see, we'll see. One thing is for sure, we need to get you into the shop. That will help clear your head."

"I am really looking forward to that." Ally smiled as she thought of all of the time she had spent in her grandmother's handmade, gourmet chocolate and coffee shop as a child. The quaint shop served as a place to disappear from the world, and let go of all of her troubles, past and present. She had loved working with her grandmother in the shop and when she had first graduated from college she took a chocolatier's course with the hopes of opening her own chocolate shop. But soon after completing the course she met her husband and her well laid plans were put on hold.

"Good, because there's plenty to do. My gift basket business has really taken off." She paused a moment and met Ally's eyes. "I could really use the help."

Ally drew a breath in surprise at her grandmother's clear request. Although Blue River was a small country town, Charlotte's handmade chocolates had been very popular for years and were in increasing demand. Charlotte had started the shop as a coffee shop, gradually she began experimenting with making chocolates and what started off as a hobby soon blossomed into a flourishing passion and business. "Why didn't you tell me? I would have come to visit sooner."

"Because I don't just want you to come to visit, Ally. I want you to come to stay." Charlotte shook her head. "I'm getting older, darling, I need to rest."

"Don't even talk like that, Mee-Maw!" Ally narrowed her eyes. A wave of dread consumed her. The very thought of her grandmother reaching an age where she felt less capable left her heart fluttering.

"Calm down, calm down, it's not like I'm going to kick it tomorrow." Charlotte laughed. "I'm just saying it would be nice to have the help. Business is growing and you can help expand it further."

Ally stared at her with parted lips and widened eyes. She wasn't quite sure how to process what her grandmother was saying. "You want me to move back here?"

"Would that be so terrible?" Her grandmother looked into her eyes. "You were happy here once."

"I was just a kid. Of course I was happy here," Ally said. "I don't know. I mean, of course I want to help, but I do have a life in the city, my job..."

"Which you hate." Charlotte raised an eyebrow.

"Well, I don't hate it but it's a bit boring." Ally frowned.

"A bit?" Charlotte grinned. "I know that you

feel like you're wasting your time there. Life is about passion, not the numbers on a paycheck. Listen Ally, I'm not asking you to stay now. I just want you to think about what you want in the future. I had always assumed, well hoped, you would take over the shop, but if that's not something you want, that's okay. It's your life, sweetie, and you've got to live it the way you choose. I'm thinking about my future, too, and I need to know if I need to think about someone else taking over the shop."

"I do want to take over the shop, absolutely. I just hate the idea of you not running it." Ally's mind spun with all of the thoughts that hadn't even been on her mind when she first arrived in town. It was difficult to think of her grandmother getting older. Ally felt as if she was the type of woman that was too strong and fierce to ever truly age. "Let me think about it, okay?"

"Sure." She gave Ally's hand a squeeze. "Just remember you don't have to do anything anybody else wants you to do. You don't have to be anybody but who you are. That oaf of an ex-husband had your head turned around. Now it's time to think about what you really want."

Ally squeezed her grandmother's hand in return. She smiled warmly at her. Her grandmother's words could be harsh, but they were always true. Daniel had insisted that she give up her dream of being a chocolatier and go to college, that she get her masters in business. It was all part of their five year plan before having children. He was determined that they would be wealthy. Ally understood the logic, but it did go against her values to some degree. Still, she had fully committed to their plan. What wasn't part of that plan was Daniel's roaming eye and his neglect, and most importantly the fact that they were never ever really suited for each other. She grimaced as she recalled the final arguments they went through.

"Thanks, Mee-Maw, I needed to hear that."

Charlotte gave her a kind smile. "It hurts, baby, don't let anyone tell you it doesn't. But it does get easier. It gets easier a lot faster when you let someone new into your life."

"No, absolutely not, no way, Mee-Maw. I'm not interested." Ally looked at her with a stern frown. "You know I love you, and I respect you, but please do not get in the middle of my romantic life."

"Would I ever even consider it?" Charlotte's mouth formed into an innocent circle and she fluttered her hand at her chest. "Really Ally. What would make you worry about that?"

Ally arched her eyebrow. "Maybe prom?"

"Well, that was different."

"Not at all." Ally crossed her arms and fixed her grandmother with a stubborn glare.

"Very different. Brent was who you should have gone with. I just helped him out."

"Mee-Maw, I mean it." Ally set her cup of tea down and yawned. "I'm a little worn out from the drive."

"You take a rest. I'm going to take Arnold for

a walk."

Ally tried not to giggle. Her grandmother always took Arnold for walks. Most of the neighbors were used to it, but some still gawked. Yes, they lived in the country, but Charlotte was the only one who had a pot-belly pig for a pet. Ally gave her grandmother a quick hug. Then she headed for her room. The cottage was only two bedrooms. One had been Ally's for as long as she could remember. It was painted a strange shade of purple that she had picked out when she was six. It was a gorgeous color to her then. Now Ally wasn't sure what to call it. Her bed was just as she had left it, with a thick quilt sewn by her great-grandmother spread across it.

Charlotte embraced tradition in their family, from heirlooms to etiquette. However, she was not too strict when it came to the choices that Ally made. The walls of Ally's room were still hung with clippings and memorabilia from her high school years. As Ally sat down on the foot of her bed, Peaches jumped up beside her. Ally stroked the cat's fur. Her eyes swept around the room. In many ways it felt like a time capsule. She remembered spending hours dreaming about what it would be like to run away to the city. She thought her dreams would come true there. She never imagined that one day she would be curled up in her king-sized bed in her luxury apartment weeping for the simplicity of her childhood.

Ally sighed and walked over to the dresser. She still stored her country clothes in it. While living in the city she had acquired a more refined taste, only because she felt as if she embarrassed Daniel in her denim and flannel. She began to realize that her grandmother was right. She had changed so much of herself to please Daniel. Maybe being back home for a while would give her the opportunity to find herself again. She changed into some comfortable clothes and then settled back in her bed. She stretched out. Immediately she was assaulted by tiny paws and a fluffy head. Peaches bumped her head against Ally's chin and rubbed her cheek across Ally's. Ally smiled and nuzzled her right back. One good thing had come out of the city, her best feline friend.

"I know you're glad to be here, too. Lots of fat rats to chase." She scratched lightly at the top of the cat's head. Peaches purred. She flicked her tail with delight. "I guess we'll just have to see how we both like it here. Maybe it is time for a change."

As she laid back and closed her eyes, Ally felt a tug on her heart. Her childhood home held a lot of beautiful memories, but it also held a lot of painful ones. In particular the memory of her mother's battle with illness. She and Ally had moved back in with Charlotte as she went through treatment. Ally had been too young to really understand, but she had felt the tension and sorrow in the home. Charlotte had transformed all of that by making their last days together one of celebration and joy. Ally still felt that subtle ache though. Her grandmother had been there for her every single day of her life since her mother passed, which kept Ally from feeling too lost, but she did wish her mother had been there as well.

As she struggled to clear her mind and fall asleep Ally felt the comfort of her great-grandmother's quilt over her, and the warmth and love contained in the walls of the cottage washed over her. She might not be able to decide if she was going to move back or not, but in that moment she knew that she was exactly where she needed to be.

Chapter Two

Ally's eyes fluttered open before she realized what had drawn her out of sleep. Then the thick, spicy scent wafted beneath her nostrils. The air filled with the delicious aroma of her grandmother's specialty coffee, made only the way her grandmother could. For a few more minutes she lay curled up in her blanket. She felt embraced by the house, its scents, and its memories. There was something incredibly soothing about being back home. With a snail's pace she unfurled from her blanket and padded over to her dresser. She didn't want to alert her grandmother that she was awake just yet. Instead she planned to sneak up on her with a great, big hug. She dressed in her most comfortable jeans and a loose blue and black flannel top. Embracing her comfortable style once more gave her a surge of contentment.

As Ally walked out of her room and towards the kitchen, Peaches followed right after her. She could hear her grandmother's voice drifting from the kitchen. Despite the fact that what she had to say could often border on harsh, her voice had a subtle lilt to it that came from years of singing in the church choir. Ally recalled the night that her grandmother confessed she wasn't much for religion, but she did love to sing. The confession broke down a barrier between the two of them and allowed Ally to confide that she wasn't much for religion either. It was hard for Ally to conceive of things such as miracles when her own life had a rough start. As she drew closer to the kitchen she could hear her grandmother's words.

"I am so happy that she's here. Honestly, if she hadn't come I probably would have gone up there and grabbed her by that little, brown ponytail and pulled her back myself."

Ally stifled a laugh at those words. Her grandmother often threatened to grab her by her little, brown ponytail, but she never actually did. Ally paused outside the kitchen to eavesdrop. It was wrong, but she was curious. Her grandmother nearly always told the truth, and even when she didn't, it was implied.

"I know, I know, we have to let them make their own mistakes. But my Ally is so precious, with such a big heart, and I hated to see her treated so poorly. Of course according to her they're both at fault. Phooey on that, he is a selfish, bore of a man and she deserves much better."

Her grandmother paused to listen. Ally thought about clearing her throat, but she found the conversation too amusing to interrupt. It meant a lot to her that her grandmother had such a high opinion of her. Divorce could be a very devastating thing. She had lost most of her friends in the city because they were mainly couple friends and were mostly Daniel's friends first. The places they would frequent became off limits to her out of fear of the questions about where Daniel was and how they were doing. It wasn't that she was ashamed, she just didn't want to deal with it.

"I know. Yes. I've already got a few lined up. I'll find somebody perfect."

At that Ally's heart jolted. What did she mean by that? She hoped her grandmother wasn't even considering the idea of setting her up. She listened closely, with the hope that she would hear more clues about what her grandmother was up to. Before she could, Peaches let out a yowl and headed for her food dish in the middle of the kitchen.

"Oh, good morning, Ally. I have to go, Greta, love to you." She hung up the phone, which was still attached to the wall, and turned to face Ally. "How are you today, sweetie?" Ally noticed the pinched corners of her lips. She could tell that her grandmother was trying to hide her guilt.

"Ready for some coffee." Ally tried to act as if she had just walked out of her room. She stroked Peaches' back and then poured some food into her dish. "Thanks for all of this."

"Just think, you could have this every morning!" Charlotte grinned as she poured Ally a cup of coffee.

"They have coffee in the city." Warmth filled Ally's smile.

"But, do they have Mee-Maws?" Charlotte wiggled her eyebrows.

"No, that they don't." Ally laughed.

"Sit, sit, I have so much to tell you!" Charlotte's eyes glowed with excitement as she sat down across from Ally. Ally smiled with anticipation, she had been so caught up in her failed marriage over the last few months that she and her grandmother had not had time to just talk about trivial things. Her grandmother was not a gossip. She made a point of telling everyone that tried to share juicy tidbits with her that she did not engage in such behavior. But when it was just her and Ally she let everything she knew spill. She trusted Ally not to spread the information or use it against anyone.

Charlotte's shop had become the pulse point of their small town. While other shops came and went, hers remained. People were very familiar with it. It was where they went to for their afternoon coffee and the first place they turned to during weddings and special events, as her chocolates were well-known far and wide. People were also very familiar with the fact that Charlotte would often put out free samples. The more bustle in the shop, the happier Charlotte was.

"Like what?" Ally blew a light breath across the surface of her coffee. She immersed herself in the scent.

"Like Jim Douglas got married to Mary Smith." Charlotte squealed with excitement. "I never thought it would happen!"

"Those two have been dating for years!" Ally laughed. "I'm glad they finally went through with it."

"It was a huge ceremony, and guess what?" Her eyes sparkled with pride.

"What?"

"They decided to have a four-tiered chocolate wedding cake and asked me to make it! That was a learning experience!" She laughed.

"Wow! That must have been fun. Did you take pictures?"

"Tons!" She smiled. "I'll show you later."

"I'm so happy for them."

"At least I got to see one wedding." Charlotte took a quick sip of her coffee.

"All right, Mee-Maw, let's not start this again." Ally cringed.

"I'm just saying, that weddings are important. And I know that it's the bride's day and she should get to choose, but it would have been nice if I had been invited." Charlotte tapped the table lightly with her cup.

"Mee-Maw, no one was invited. We eloped. Remember?" Ally avoided looking directly at her grandmother.

"Oh, I remember. I remember very clearly."

"And we agreed not to talk about it anymore?" Ally looked over at her with a sigh. "What does it matter now, anyway?"

Charlotte nodded a little. "You're right, I'm sorry, Ally, it was insensitive of me to bring that up. You know me, always saying what's on my mind before I think it through."

"It's okay. What about Brent, have you heard anything new about him?" Ally tried to change the subject. Her heart ached a little with regret. She knew that she had hurt her grandmother when she didn't involve her in the wedding. It was a spur of the moment decision. Ally had barely been involved in it herself.

"Brent has that auto repair shop going pretty well. He's still single." She winked at Ally. "As far as I know he's been staying out of trouble. I haven't seen that much of him since I hired Connor to help me with the deliveries."

"Connor Troy?" Ally sat back in her chair.

"He needed a job, and I needed a driver when we started getting frequent orders for deliveries to the city." Charlotte shrugged. "I don't know why those two boys can't just shake hands and end the silly feud between their families."

"Not everyone forgives so easily." Ally finished her coffee.

"We better head in soon. You're coming with me right?" Charlotte picked up the coffee cups.

"Yes, I can't wait to get my hands sticky!"

Chapter Three

Everything was within walking distance in Blue River. It was one of the things Ally liked most about it. She often spent time wandering as a child. At the time she knew who lived in every house, who owned every shop, and when something was obviously different. One of the most exciting times was when a new family moved into town. She was only eight at the time, but it was a little shocking to her that new people could simply move in. She was so accustomed to a certain group of people, that these strangers fascinated her. They were only from the next town over, but they might as well have been from the planet Mars to Ally.

As she walked beneath the flowering trees that lined the sidewalk Ally drew in a deep breath. It was always interesting to her that the air seemed more nourishing outside of the city. In the back of her mind she attributed it to more trees, but she knew in reality it was because she was more relaxed. In the city there was always so much pressure, to be someone, to do something, she never found a moment to just take a stroll.

"Look at that." Charlotte clucked her tongue. "Can you believe that someone would do that to Vivian's house?"

Ally looked up at the towering Victorian style home. It was three stories with little turrets and round rooms that drew everyone's attention. Vivian's house, as it was known by everyone in town, was one of the largest. When Ally was a little girl she viewed it as a castle, or at the very least a mansion. Now she knew that it was just a large house, but it still held a magical quality for her. However, whoever had purchased the home must not have found it very magical as they were practically tearing it down and replacing the majority of the exterior.

"And the noise." Charlotte shook her head. "It scares my customers away. I wish people would just appreciate things for what they are instead of always trying to improve something that was beautiful to begin with."

Ally smiled at her thoughts. Her grandmother had an open mind, but she did like certain things to stay the same. She valued the past almost as much as she savored the present.

"I'm sure that it doesn't keep your customers away." Ally nudged her lightly with her elbow. "Nothing has ever kept your customers away."

"Okay, true, they are loyal and business is growing. But still, who can enjoy their coffee while listening to that racket?"

"Hopefully, they will finish soon." It was a little disappointing to Ally to see that progress even reached the little town, but she reminded herself that some change could be good.

As they walked up to the shop, Ally smiled at the sight of it. It only had one door and one large front window to announce its presence. It didn't need a sign, as everyone knew that the shop was there. Beside the door on the brick between the chocolate shop and a boutique was a bulletin board. Charlotte had hung it there for anyone to post anything of interest. The goal was to generate foot traffic around the chocolate shop and it had worked. Now, if anyone wanted to know what was happening in town they would head straight for the bulletin board.

The large, front window had a delicious display of the various handmade chocolates, candies, cookies, cakes and muffins that Charlotte created. Fond memories flooded through Ally's mind. She had spent the vast majority of her childhood with her nose pressed against the window. In exchange for her help around the shop sweeping up, cleaning counters, and making small deliveries, Ally was paid one chocolate of her choice. It was always the hardest choice that Ally had to make.

Charlotte unlocked the door to the shop and stepped inside. Ally followed after her. As Charlotte flipped on the light in the front area of the shop, Ally watched the decorations around the room spring to life. Charlotte liked to collect unique, handmade pieces of art. She had many wooden clocks, wooden toys, and a variety of masks hung or displayed throughout the shop. It was her way of supporting local artists. Ally took a moment to admire a piece she had not seen before.

"Where did you get this?" Ally asked. It was a tiny, wooden hummingbird created with such delicate detail that Ally couldn't even picture the blade that could have made it.

"Oh, actually that was given to me." Charlotte opened up the register for the day. "There's a new detective in town, and I guess he noticed the decorations in here. I think it was meant to be a kind gesture, but I don't know."

"What do you mean? It's beautiful." Ally gazed at the piece with admiration as she set it back down.

"There's just something about him that doesn't seem genuine. He was very friendly at first, when he gave me the bird, but he is very offish to me now." Charlotte shrugged. "Maybe I'm wrong. I've been wrong before. He just doesn't seem to fit together right."

"He's from out of town?"

"Yes. He's only been here for a few weeks." Charlotte gestured for Ally to follow her back into the kitchen. There was a large window in the kitchen that faced the inside of the shop. It gave customers the opportunity to observe some of the chocolate making and intricate decorating process.

"Maybe you just need to get to know him." Ally smiled. "This town isn't too kind to outsiders."

"Maybe." Charlotte sighed. Then she grinned at Ally. "I can tell you this much about him. He's way too pretty not to be in the movies."

"What?" Ally laughed.

"I'm serious, he's got those Hollywood looks. I don't know what he's doing here, but he's got all of the local ladies in a tizzy to get his attention." She clucked her tongue. "I try to tell them there's a lot more to a man than some straight teeth and some bright eyes, but they don't listen."

"Hmm, sounds like you've noticed just how handsome he is too, Mee-Maw." Ally giggled.

"Hush! He's young enough to be my grandson." She pointed out some mixing bowls on the counter. "You know what you need to do, my darling?" Charlotte smiled, displaying her beautiful teeth. "You need to make something. Anything. Choose any recipe you like. If we don't have the ingredients that you need, then we will get them. Okay?"

"You're right, as usual." Ally walked over to a large, wooden box. It stored all of the recipes that had been handed down through her family, as well as new ones that had been added. Ally began sorting through the recipe box. A few years before Ally had transcribed the recipes onto the computer. However, she still preferred to feel the old recipe cards with her fingertips. They were thinning with age and smelled faintly of vanilla and chocolate.

There was one recipe that Ally had always

wanted to try. It was a triple chocolate muffin recipe. There was nothing more cathartic to her than losing herself in one of her grandmother's treasured recipes. They were filled with more than just delectable taste. Each ingredient was lovingly written on the card and Ally liked to think that she could feel the emotions that her grandmother had felt as she wrote it. This particular recipe felt like it had been invented to be comfort food. Ally could sure use a little bit of that.

"Look at these, Ally." Charlotte smiled as she held up a chocolate from the gift box she had been creating.

"Cute," Ally said with a smile as she looked at the small chocolate rose.

"I made them especially for a special customer," Charlotte said as she handed it to Ally. "Have a taste."

"It smells delicious," Ally said as she took the rose from her grandmother. She placed it gently in her mouth.

"Salted caramel," Charlotte explained as Ally

savored the taste.

"Yum!" Ally exclaimed as the slightly salty sweetness coated her mouth.

"Now get back to it," Charlotte commanded. "I feel like muffins." Ally retreated to her bench with a smile. She had missed spending time with her grandmother.

"Hello?" A familiar voice drifted in from the back door of the shop.

"Connor!" Charlotte smiled as he walked in. "I almost have the order ready. Did you bring the flowers?"

"Yes, I have them right here." He held up a bouquet of pale pink roses. Ally pretended not to notice him. However, out of the corner of her eye she was paying him very close attention. She noticed that his blonde curls were as tight and unruly as they had always been. He was also just as tall and lanky, all elbows and knees as her grandmother had once called him. She also detected that his voice had deepened. Connor was a late bloomer when they were in school together.

He had a squeaky voice right up until graduation.

"Oh, are they light pink?" Charlotte clucked her tongue. "I thought they would be dark pink. I bought the wrong shade of ribbon. It's supposed to match the flowers. I don't have a shade that light."

"I could run to the fabric store for you." Ally offered her help without looking at Connor.

"No, that's okay, you're in the middle of the recipe. I'll go get it. You keep Connor company while I'm gone."

Ally looked up in time to see her grandmother wink at her before she disappeared to the front of the shop.

"Ally. It's good to see you." Connor offered her an awkward smile. They hadn't really known each other that well, but had nothing against each other either.

"You too, Connor. It's been a long time." Ally flashed him a smile, but refocused on mixing the ingredients right away.

Connor leaned against the counter beside her and watched as she folded the ingredients together. Mixing had always been Ally's favorite step in a recipe. It was when all of the parts came together to form a deep, rich liquid that always had a lovely aroma.

"That looks good."

"I hope it will taste good." Ally laughed.

"Are you back in town for good?" Connor sounded almost hopeful.

"No, just visiting. For now." Ally recalled her grandmother's request to make the move back. She hadn't thought that much about it yet. It did feel wonderful to be back home. But would that novelty wear off with time?

"This place could use you." Connor rapped his knuckles on the counter. "Seems to me that everyone is getting crankier and crankier. You always have such a good attitude."

"Really?" Ally glanced over at him. She hadn't realized that he had paid that much attention to her. "I mean, I try to see things in a positive way."

"That's good." Connor nodded. "There's enough stress and sadness in the world. We need more sunshine."

Ally tried not to giggle at being compared to sunshine. She thought that Connor might be trying just a little too hard to compliment her. "What's been happening lately?"

"Not too much. Just weddings, and divorces, and more weddings." Connor laughed. Then he cleared his throat. "I'm sorry, Ally, I wasn't talking about you."

Ally furrowed a brow. "You know about the divorce?"

"Well, you're not wearing a ring," Connor pointed out. Ally looked down at the ghost-white skin where her ring had once been.

"You're right, I'm not. I guess that's been going around a little?"

"Yes. I have to say that I'm glad I never took the plunge myself. I'm waiting for the right person

I guess." He shrugged. "I can only hope that she's waiting for me, too."

"That's really sweet, Connor." Ally smiled.

"Do you think we could get a drink after work?" Connor blurted out the question. Ally was blindsided by it. She hadn't expected him to invite her out.

"Uh, well. Sure." Ally shrugged. "Maybe. Let me see how I'm feeling at the end of the day, okay?"

"Great." Connor smiled as if she had just agreed to marry him. "Do you need anything?"

"Could you grab me that spoon over there?" Ally pointed to a long handled spoon amid an assortment of spoons.

Connor plucked the spoon out of the jar and handed it to her. "What are you making?"

"Triple chocolate muffins."

"Oh, I can't wait to try one of those." Connor grinned. "If you'll share that is."

"I'll share." Ally smiled. "If they come out

edible."

"They will come out delicious!" Charlotte said as she walked back into the kitchen with a length of ribbon dangling from her hand. "Perfect match!" She smiled triumphantly. "Now, Connor you need to get this over there quickly because it's already late."

"I've already put the address in the GPS. Don't worry, I'll be quick." Connor smiled and waved to Ally as he walked out through the back door with Charlotte. Ally nodded back, but she had already been drawn back into the swirl and scent of the mixture in the bowl. When Charlotte returned she had a wide grin.

"So, you're going out with Connor after work."

"What?" Ally nearly dropped the spoon into the mixture. "No, I said maybe I would have a drink with him."

"Maybe that should be a yes. He's a very good man. He's always willing to help, even more than what his job entails." Charlotte stuck her finger in the mixture and took a taste. "Mm. This is a very good start."

"Mee-Maw, I'm sure Connor is a very nice fellow, but I'm not interested in anything more than sharing a drink, if I even do that. You promised you would stay out of my love life, remember?" Ally watched as her grandmother added another dash of vanilla to the mixture.

"I didn't exactly promise. But I appreciate your opinion on the matter." Charlotte winked at her.

"I'm serious, Mee-Maw, I just don't want to even think about it right now."

"Shh, just stir." Charlotte patted Ally's shoulder and walked away.

Ally lost herself in the swirl, and then the cupcake tins, and then the layers of chocolate batter. As soon as she had them out of the oven she started helping her grandmother make some tiramisu, white chocolate truffles. After that she spent the rest of the afternoon helping her grandmother design and price different gift box combinations in-between serving customers.

When Ally finally glanced up at one of the wooden clocks she was shocked to find it was almost closing time. Connor still hadn't returned and she felt a bit of a sting that he hadn't come back to have a drink with her.

"Connor still isn't back?" Charlotte shook her head as she stepped into the kitchen. "I've tried to reach him on his cell phone. I guess he got caught up with something."

"Are you sure?" Ally frowned. "Is it normal for him to just not come back? Doesn't he still have the delivery van?"

"Sometimes he has errands to run. I don't often need the van because I walk most places so I let him use the van to drive home and back and anything else he needs during the day. I don't pay him a large salary so that makes up for it some." She sniffed the muffins. "Oh, Ally I've never smelled anything so delicious."

"You're just being nice." Ally shook her head.

"I'm not, I mean it." Charlotte plucked a crumb off the top of one of the muffins and popped it into her mouth. "Yummy!"

Ally couldn't help but smile with pride. She didn't think that she would ever be able to bake like her grandmother did, but it was nice to get her approval.

"I guess it's time to close." Ally walked over to the sink to wash the muffin tins.

"I'm sorry that Connor didn't come back for that drink." Charlotte picked up a towel to help dry off the tins.

"It's okay. I probably would have said no anyway." Ally shrugged. She gazed towards the back door. A part of her knew that she wouldn't have. It did hurt just a tiny bit that he wasn't as interested as she had thought.

Chapter Four

When Ally and Charlotte arrived back at the cottage that night, Charlotte went to the living room to watch a few of her favorite shows. Ally decided to retreat to her bedroom and curl up with the book she had brought with her. Peaches jumped right up onto the bed with her. Ally snuggled her close.

"Well, I guess some things will never change, Peaches. I might not be ready to have a new relationship, but I still have that wish to be desired." She scratched behind the cat's ear. "Life can be a little lonely. Good thing I have you." She placed a light peck on the top of the cat's head and then picked up her book. She had to read to keep her mind from wandering to what Daniel might be doing at that moment. The book was a good distraction from the 'what ifs' that tended to plague her when she had a moment to think. After reading for some time the words began to blur. Ally felt the need to rest. Her mind spun with dizziness. She closed her eyes and drifted off.

Deep in her sleep Ally heard pounding. It made her think of the Victorian house that was being fixed up. Somewhere in her slumber she was aware that they were too far from that house for that to be the source of the pounding. Another round of heavy knocks drew her fully from her sleep. Once she was awake she knew that the pounding was coming from her bedroom door. Ally jumped up out of her bed in a daze. Was it her grandmother? Was something wrong? Before she got to the door it flung open. Charlotte burst through.

"Mee-Maw?"

Charlotte stood before her with tears in her eyes. "Oh Ally, it's horrible, just horrible."

"What is it? Are you hurt? What's wrong?" Ally's heart raced with fear.

"It's Connor. They found him." Charlotte could hardly get another word out. As her grandmother struggled to speak Ally knew that the situation had to be dire. She reached out and hugged her grandmother.

"It's good they found him, isn't it?" Her voice trembled with foresight of what her grandmother would say.

"No, he's gone, Ally. They found him beside a dumpster, dead." Charlotte clasped a hand over her mouth in horror.

The words struck Ally so hard that she had to hold onto her grandmother to keep her balance. Was she serious?

"But I just saw him," she protested. "Are they sure it's Connor?"

"They're sure. That must be why he didn't come back from the delivery. While we were talking about him, he was probably already dead." She shook her head. "I feel awful. You were right, we should have checked on him!"

"Mee-Maw, you couldn't have known." Ally was still in shock herself. Of all the things that she thought might happen on her visit to her grandmother's home she didn't think that someone dying would be one of them. "Do they know what happened? Did he have some kind of health condition?"

Charlotte drew a deep breath and looked into Ally's eyes. "No darling, he was shot, he was murdered."

"Murdered?" Ally's eyes widened. In all the time that she had lived in the city she had never known anyone who had been murdered. Certainly, growing up in their small, country town she had never known of any murders. It was shocking enough that someone she had just spoken to the day before was dead, but to think that he was murdered was unfathomable.

"I know, it's terrible." Charlotte shook her head. "I don't even know what to think."

"Do they know who did it?"

"Not as far as I know." Charlotte shuddered. "I guess we'll have to go into town and open up the shop. I'm sure we'll find out every detail then."

Ally nodded. "I'll get dressed." Her voice was

barely audible. She still struggled to process Connor's murder. Once she was alone, Ally dressed in silence. Even Peaches, who would normally be begging for breakfast, seemed to understand that something terrible had happened. She didn't make a sound until Ally opened the door and walked out into the hall. Peaches weaved her body through Ally's legs, nearly causing her to trip.

"Peaches!" Ally frowned. "I don't need any of that this morning."

Peaches pranced off to the kitchen. Ally followed after her more reluctantly. She fed her and filled her water. Then she looked up as her grandmother walked into the kitchen.

"Do you want me to make some coffee?" Ally offered.

"No. No, not today. I think we'd better just go into the shop. I imagine that the police will want to speak with us and see where Connor worked," her voice was subdued. Ally sensed that she was still trying to make sense of the news. She walked over to her grandmother and hugged her warmly.

"I'm sorry, Mee-Maw."

"I just hate to see such a young person…" Her voice caught in her throat. She hugged Ally back with a tight embrace. "Enough of this or we'll never get out of here."

Ally nodded. They walked towards the shop in silence. There were others outside, some watering their grass, some biking or walking, but they did not wave to each other as they normally would. No one shouted an awkward good morning. It was not a good morning, and word had gotten around fast. Charlotte unlocked the shop and they walked inside. Ally felt uneasy as she recalled the last conversation she had with Connor. Had she been kind enough? Had she missed some kind of sign that he was afraid for his life? She didn't think so. It seemed so odd to her that a life could be wiped out so suddenly.

"Have a muffin," Charlotte insisted. "We'll need our strength today."

Ally knew that she was right, but the very idea

of eating made her stomach churn.

"I will, but isn't there something I can do to keep myself busy for a bit?" Ally frowned. "I need to clear my head."

"Sure. You can tie some bows for the gift baskets. There are supplies in the top drawer by the tall cabinet." Charlotte drifted into the kitchen. Ally gathered the supplies and began creating bows out of the ribbons. Her mind kept analyzing Connor's presence, his grin, the excitement in his eyes. She wished she had given him the same attention.

The bell above the door of the shop tinkled quietly. Ally lifted her eyes from the bows she had been tying to see two men. Both were neatly dressed and both had small badges clipped to their belts. Ally felt her heart jump as she realized that they must be police detectives. She recognized one of them right away, Julian Borron. Ally had a huge crush on him throughout high school, but he was a few grades higher than her and had never even looked in her direction. He had jet black hair and clear blue eyes. Her entire sophomore year was wasted on dreaming about dating him. Of course after he graduated she found a new crush, but it was still a little embarrassing to think about.

"Ally?" Julian smiled at her, his blue eyes flashed with recognition. "It's Ally right?"

Ally felt a strange flutter of excitement at the fact that he remembered her name. "Yes."

"Do you remember me? We went to high school together." He walked towards the counter.

"Yes, I remember, Julian." Ally smiled at him.

"This is my partner, Luke Elm. We're investigating the death of Connor Troy." He glanced past her towards the back of the shop. "Is your grandmother here?"

Ally's gaze wandered over to the other detective. His hair was light brown and a bit longer than most detectives. It had a subtle wave in it. His eyes were a sharp shade of blue, bright and inquisitive. He had flawless features with high cheekbones, a strong jaw, and lips just plump enough to distract her.

"Sure, let me get her." Ally forced her mind back to the matter at hand. She stepped into the back to find her grandmother with her hands wrist deep in batter. "Mee-Maw, there are two detectives out front. I think they must have some questions about Connor."

"Oh dear." Charlotte raised her hands to show that they were covered in sticky batter. "Can you talk to them for a minute while I clean up?"

"Sure." Ally turned back towards the door, then paused. "Don't be long."

"I won't."

When Ally stepped back into the front room, she noticed the two men speaking softly to one another. Her heart skipped a beat. She had always struggled a bit with being nervous around police.

"She'll be out in just a minute." Ally rested her hands on the counter.

Luke met her eyes directly. She was so

distracted by the sight of those beautiful eyes that she must have missed the question that he was asking.

"Ally?" His voice was stern.

"Hmm?" She smiled.

"Did you speak with Connor Troy yesterday?" Luke frowned.

"Oh yes, I did. Right before he left to make a delivery for my grandmother."

"What was the last thing you and Connor talked about?" He continued to hold her gaze with his own.

"Oh uh, we had talked about getting a drink after work."

"You were dating?" Julian jumped in with the question. His eyes searched Ally's with an intensity that surprised her.

"No," Ally answered a little too swiftly. "I just got into town the day before. We were just going to get a drink as friends. Actually, I hadn't said yes, I said we'd talk about it when he got back and it would depend on how I was feeling."

"So, you knew that he should have come back last night?" Luke drew her attention back to him.

"Well sure. I mean, he should have come back before we closed."

"And when he didn't?" Luke made a note on his small notepad.

"When he didn't Mee-Maw, I mean Charlotte, called his cell phone. He didn't answer." She sighed. "We didn't know anything was wrong. I just figured he'd got caught up somewhere with someone, or maybe had decided to head home for the night instead of coming back to the shop."

"Maybe you had upset him by turning down his offer for a drink?" Luke raised an eyebrow. "Is that possible?"

"I didn't turn him down." Ally studied Luke more intently. "It's not like I was rude to him or anything. I just said maybe."

"Well, that's not really an answer, is it?" Ally noticed a hint of discomfort in Luke's voice. She couldn't quite place what emotion was affecting the way he spoke. She did find it odd however.

"So, after you turned him down for the drink he left right away?" Julian interrupted.

Ally frowned as she looked between the two men. She was beginning to feel as if she was being bullied into agreeing to something she didn't do.

"Listen, Connor and I went to school together. My grandmother was trying to stir something up between us. I didn't say yes or no to the drink and I was certainly not mean. Yes, he left after that in a hurry, but that was only because the delivery was late."

"Why was the delivery late?" Luke made another note.

"It needed a certain color ribbon and my grandmother did not have it on hand so she had to go to the fabric shop to pick it up." Ally gestured to the slip of paper she had placed on the counter. "All of the information about the order and delivery address is there for you to look at."

"So, you were alone with Connor?" Luke drew her attention back to him again. Ally noticed that his square features were even sharper with tension. She was getting a little confused by the way he was questioning her.

"Yes."

"Why didn't you go to the fabric store?"

"I was in the middle of making triple chocolate muffins," Ally said. "I really wish that I could help out more with this, but the truth is, I didn't notice anything unusual about the way Connor was acting. I have no idea why someone would want to hurt him."

"Sometimes people know more than they realize." Luke tapped his pen lightly on his notepad.

Ally found it difficult to focus on what he was saying.

"Ally?" Luke pressed.

Charlotte stepped out from the back of the shop. "Detectives." Charlotte offered them both a winning smile.

"Hi Ms. Charlotte." Julian returned her smile. "Do you know Luke?"

"Ah yes." She offered a tight smile to Luke. "A very talented craftsman."

Luke only nodded at her in return. He looked at Charlotte for a moment, then returned his attention to Ally.

"Did Connor mention any arguments he'd had? Any financial trouble?"

"No. We didn't talk much."

Luke turned his attention to Charlotte. "Did he mention any of that to you?"

"No. Connor was a good boy."

"A grown man." Luke narrowed his eyes. "He was in his twenties."

"You, young man, are still a boy to me," Charlotte bit her words back. Ally cringed at the sharp tone she took with Luke, but it did not surprise her.

"Did you know his family well?" Luke continued as if her correction had no impact on him.

"As well as anyone else in this town."

Luke glanced over at Ally and then back at Charlotte. "Is it a family trait not to answer questions?"

"Excuse me?"

Ally braced herself as she waited for Charlotte to unleash a tongue-lashing. Julian stepped in before things could get any more tense.

"I think we have all of the information we need, Ms. Charlotte. Thank you for your time."

Luke scowled slightly in Julian's direction. Ally moved closer to her grandmother.

"Julian, wait just a minute." Charlotte picked up a platter from behind the counter.

"Yes?" Julian turned back.

"You know better than to walk out of here with an empty stomach." She smiled sweetly at him. Julian grinned.

"Thanks, Ms. Charlotte." He picked up one of the cookies. Charlotte looked over at Luke. "You too, young man."

Luke shook his head. "No thanks."

Silence fell amongst them. Ally held her breath as she wondered how her grandmother would react. Luke looked between the troubled expressions and seemed to gather that he had made a mistake.

"I'd rather have one of those muffins." He cleared his throat. "If you don't mind."

Ally tried not to be amused by the timid way he looked at Charlotte. She picked up one of the triple chocolate muffins and offered it to Luke.

"It's quite rich."

"Thanks, the richer the better. We'll be in touch." He nodded to Ally and Charlotte, then turned towards the door as Julian crunched down on a cookie.

"Let's go to the auto shop," Julian said to Luke between bites.

Charlotte pulled Ally to the side. "I don't think I trust this."

"Trust what?" Ally glanced past her grandmother to the two detectives that were just walking out the door.

"Julian knows the area, but Luke isn't from around here. I don't know of any Elms that have ever lived in this town. He turned down one of my cookies. I don't trust him."

"Well, I think we're on even ground then, because he sure doesn't seem to trust us." Ally watched the two men disappear down the sidewalk.

"I'm just sick about what's happened." Charlotte wrung her hands. "I wish there was something more that we could do. I'm concerned that Luke isn't going to be as invested in finding out the truth since he is from out of town. He's probably from a place where murders happen all of the time."

"Relax, Mee-Maw I'm sure he'll do his job." Ally felt a little unsettled as well, despite coming to Luke's defense.

"But, did you see the way he acted? I don't know. It seems like he's trying to be too much of a tough guy. Hopefully Julian will take control." Charlotte sighed.

"Hopefully," Ally muttered. "I think I'm going to take a walk. Is that okay with you?"

"Sure, I doubt we'll have a huge rush this morning."

Chapter Five

Ally slipped out the back door of the shop. She could see the parking lot from it. She waited until the two detectives were in their car, then she stepped all the way outside. As Charlotte had predicted, the parking lot was empty with no sign of filling up any time soon. Once the detectives were out of the driveway Ally made her way through the backyard of the neighboring house. Even though the detectives were in a car, she knew that she would likely beat them across town. There were stop signs and traffic lights on the road, and she knew every short cut to get across town as quickly as possible.

When Ally emerged behind the library she noticed that their car was just turning down the street towards the auto shop. She gave them a few minutes to drive into the parking lot, park, and get out. Then she crossed the road and headed to the shop as well. There was a small opening between the auto shop and the convenience store that was next to it. That was where the dumpster was. Ally crept along the outside of the auto shop and paused a few feet from the corner. She could hear Julian and Luke talking.

"It doesn't make much sense does it?" Luke asked.

"What do you expect, a step-by-step plan?" Julian's voice was coated with annoyance. "I think that it is pretty plain to see what happened here. Someone was after him, and caught up with him."

"I don't know. I mean, don't you think it's strange that he went out for a delivery and didn't return, but neither Charlotte or Ally thought to call the police to report him missing?"

Ally tensed at the tone in Luke's voice. Was he really suspecting her or her grandmother of being involved in some way in the murder? She narrowed her eyes. Maybe her grandmother was right about him. The way he was acting was very suspicious.

"Not really. You don't know the way of this town. People are in everybody's business but they're also not, they respect each other's privacy. So, Connor didn't come back from the delivery, that didn't make him missing. Maybe it made him drunk at the bar, or hooking up with someone's wife, but it didn't make him missing. People don't call the police for just anything around here."

"If you say so." Luke shook his head. "Something doesn't seem right though."

"Trust me, you're barking up the wrong tree. I already have a pretty good idea of who did this."

"You do?" Luke glanced over at him.

Ally leaned a little closer to be sure that she was hearing Julian clearly.

"There's a history with Connor's family and the family of the man who owns the auto shop, Brent. It goes way back. Lots of bad blood."

"What kind of bad blood?"

"Just the usual land squabble that turned into one family hating the other family and little fights and romantic issues between the generations. Basically, they irritate each other." Ally heard his voice draw a little closer to her and she ducked back against the side of the building. She didn't want to be caught snooping, that would only make the already apparently suspicious Luke even more suspicious.

"Well, that sounds like a lead to look into." Luke cleared his throat. "It certainly doesn't look like a calculated murder, it looks like a crime of passion or rage."

Ally started to turn away as it sounded like the two detectives were headed in her direction. Before she could, she heard a deep growl. She recognized the sound right away. Peaches darted out from behind her and headed straight towards the dumpster. The cat's fast motion sent a mouse running for its life, and Julian running after the cat.

"Not so fast you little pest! No contaminating the crime scene," he said with a laugh as he scooped up the cat. Ally couldn't stop herself from chasing after her feline friend. She boldly walked out in front of the two detectives.

"That's my cat, Peaches!" She frowned and held her arms out for the cat. Julian turned to look at Ally while scratching at the cat's neck.

"Did she escape?"

"Yes. I'm sorry." Ally took the cat back from him. She avoided looking directly at Luke, after overhearing his opinion about her and her grandmother she didn't want to give him any more reason to suspect her.

"So, she slipped out of the shop and just happened to follow us all the way here?" Luke crossed the few feet between them. He reached out and pet Peaches' orange fur. Ally noticed that he didn't wear any ring

"She wasn't at the shop. She was at my grandmother's cottage. We must have left the door open when we left this morning." She shifted the cat in her grasp. "She's always escaping."

"Maybe you should keep better track of her," Luke suggested. Ally accidentally met his eyes. She felt like he was indicating she should have kept better track of Connor, too.

"I have her now." She gritted her teeth and turned away from him.

"Ally wait!" Julian said as he stepped closer to her. "Tell me something, did Connor mention any issues with Brent Nissle?"

"Brent?" Ally looked at him as she tried to act surprised. "Why?"

"You two dated, didn't you?" Julian smiled. Ally was shocked that he would remember something like that. Maybe Julian had paid more attention to her in high school than she realized.

"A little in high school. A long time ago."

"Huh. So you dated Brent in the past, and Connor asked you out for a drink? Maybe Brent didn't like that too much?" Luke's voice hardened as if he was already convinced of what he was suspecting.

Julian walked closer to her. As he did Ally caught a whiff of something strange on his shirt. It wasn't a bad smell but it wasn't particularly good, maybe it was his cologne or soap.

"That is ridiculous," Ally said. "I haven't seen Brent in years, and Connor and I barely spoke. Connor asking me for a drink had nothing to do with this."

"But here you are, eavesdropping." Luke held her gaze as if he was daring her to lie about what she had been doing. "Is there a reason for that?"

"I was looking for my cat." Ally returned his gaze just as steadily. She had no qualms with lying to a man who seemed convinced that she was somehow involved in a murder. For just a second she felt a twinge of fear. Was he trying to frame her?

"You've found it." Luke patted Peaches lightly on the top of her head. Peaches hissed. She might have sensed how annoyed Luke was making Ally.

"Her. I've found her." Ally turned away with her pet. Luke might have been one of the handsomest men she had ever laid eyes on, but she didn't like the way that he spoke about her cat.

"We'll let you know if we have any more questions, Ally," Luke called after her as she walked away. Ally didn't even bother to nod or look back. She didn't want to be asked any more questions. What she wanted was to figure out what had actually happened to Connor.

Chapter Six

Ally headed back to the cottage with Peaches. She wanted to be sure that the cat wouldn't escape again. When she got there she noticed that the back door was open. She didn't remember ever opening the back door. Maybe her grandmother had opened it and in the chaos of the morning somehow it had been left open. She secured the door and then went through the rest of the cottage to make sure that everything was as it should be.

"You stay put!" Ally warned her cat. Then she left for the shop. She decided to drive in case they had any deliveries for the day. As she drove she thought about the strange way Luke behaved. He seemed to have a problem with her without even knowing her. Or maybe he was just doing his job and she was used to the friendly demeanor of most of the people in the town. When Ally returned to her grandmother's shop she found three ladies inside waiting at the counter. They chatted quietly to one another.

"I heard that it was all over a girl."

"Nonsense, Connor wasn't seeing anyone. I heard that he was involved in drugs."

"Oh yes, drugs. Drugs will always get you killed." The third woman sucked her teeth and shook her head. "It all starts at home you know. Maybe if his busybody of a mother hadn't gone and gotten herself knocked up by that other man..."

"Hello!" Ally spoke up brightly. She didn't want to hear anything more about Connor's mother's affair. The three women all turned to face Ally. One by one warm smiles appeared on their perfectly lipsticked lips.

"Ally! I didn't know you were in town."

"So sorry to hear about your marriage."

"Don't worry, dear, you're still so young, and pretty." The third woman sucked her teeth again and shook her head. "Such a shame."

"Mrs. White, Mrs. Cale, Mrs. Bing, thank you for your concern, but I'm doing just fine.

Sometimes it just doesn't work out." Ally remembered them all as the town gossips. Well, really there were many more than three, these three in particular just happened to be the most easily noticed, because they weren't exactly discreet.

"Not like in my day." Mrs. Bing shook her head. "Back then there wasn't an option for things not to work out. We got married, we stay married."

Ally opened her mouth to share her opinion, but before she could Mrs. Cale interrupted. "Oh shut it, Bessie, no one deserves to be stuck in a miserable marriage. You should know."

"My marriage was not miserable!"

"That's not what he said." Mrs. White giggled.

"What's going on out here, ladies?" Charlotte stepped out of the back with three small boxes of chocolates. Ally looked from Mrs. Bing's horrified face, to Mrs. White's all too pleased smirk, and did her best not to laugh.

"Well, I never!" Mrs. Bing snatched up her box of chocolates and stormed out of the shop.

"I heard he never." Mrs. White winked at Mrs. Cale.

"Ladies." Charlotte wagged a finger at them with playful criticism. "We mustn't gossip."

"You're right, Charlotte." Mrs. White nodded.

"Ally, could you help me in the kitchen?" Charlotte requested. "I trust you two have what you came for." She slid the small boxes towards the women.

"Oh yes, thank you so much, Charlotte." Mrs. White gushed her gratitude and snatched up her box. Mrs. Cale picked up hers as well. She spared Ally a light wink as she stepped out the door. Once they were alone Charlotte rolled her eyes.

"They're like sharks those women, they smell blood and they attack."

"I remember." Ally passed a somber gaze over her shoulder. She could recall many occasions of being treated differently because she was the child of a single mother, and then essentially an orphan.

"Don't let them get to you. Come tell me what you found out. I know you didn't just go for a walk."

Ally followed her grandmother into the kitchen. "How do you know?"

"Because you're a lot like me, Ally. I wouldn't have just gone for a walk. So, what do you know?" She looked at Ally.

"I don't know much, other than that their prime suspect is Brent Nissle."

"That doesn't surprise me. There are plenty of people that know about the problems between those families."

"And the body was found by Brent's shop." Ally sighed. "But that's not all. It seems that as suspicious as we are of Luke, he's suspicious of us, too. I don't know why, but it seems he has a problem with me. I think I made it worse because they caught me snooping."

"Oh dear. Well, that's not something to worry too much about. Listen, I'm going to work in the back for a bit. I'm going to make something special to take over to Connor's mother. Can you keep an eye on the front and tidy up a bit?"

"Sure." Ally nodded. When she stepped back into the front of the shop she settled into her old routine of wiping down all of the counters.

She swished the rag back and forth over the same spot several times.

"Are you trying to wear a hole into the counter?" Charlotte asked from just behind her. Ally jumped, despite recognizing her grandmother's voice.

"Sorry, I was just thinking."

"Thinking about what?" Charlotte frowned and took the rag from her.

"Just something that new detective, Luke, said."

"What did he say?" Charlotte walked over to the register and began rifling through the receipts.

"Julian was telling him about the bad blood between Brent's family and Connor's family. Then he accused me of knowing more about the situation than I was saying. As if I tried to play Connor against Brent, or the other way around." She shook her head.

"He accused you?" Charlotte's voice heightened with anger. "How dare he!"

"Well, not in those exact words, but it was close enough." Ally sighed. "I just hope they're not going to try to blame Brent for this without doing a thorough investigation."

"Brent's not the same boy you remember," Charlotte's tone was quiet. She set down the receipts and looked over at Ally. "Things change, people change, even in small towns, Ally."

"Not that much though," Ally stated firmly. "I don't think it's possible. At least I hope it isn't."

"I'm going to finish up in the back." Charlotte patted Ally's shoulder as she walked past. Ally managed a smile in her grandmother's direction. They could disagree on a topic and have it not be an issue, but Ally was genuinely bothered by what her grandmother had said. Did people really change that much? Could someone like Brent, a friend she had trusted, really become a killer? As Ally thought about this she lost herself in dusting and straightening the shelves. As she worked she nearly knocked over the hummingbird that Luke had given to her grandmother. It struck her that she had considered it so beautiful before, now that she had met the man who created it, she had a hard time believing that he could create something so beautiful. Maybe her grandmother was right about people changing.

The door to the shop swung open and a young woman walked in. Ally thought she looked fairly familiar, but then just about everyone in town did. She looked young enough to be finishing school.

"Amy?" Ally gasped with surprise as she recognized her.

Amelia offered a nervous smile. "It's been a

long time, Ally."

"Last time I saw you you were still in pigtails." Ally smiled at her. Then her smile faded some. She had a feeling that Amelia had an ulterior motive for the visit.

"Did you hear about Connor?" Amelia asked.

"Yes. I did." Ally frowned. "It was terrible news."

"Then I'm sure you've also spoken to the detectives." Amelia brushed her hand lightly back through her hair. "I spoke to them, too."

"I did." Ally nodded. She felt uncomfortable as she studied Amelia and wondered what she was really there for.

"They think Brent is involved. I knew they would, as soon as I heard about it." She shook her head. "I told him to settle things with Connor, to put all of this behind our families, but you know how stubborn my brother is."

"I do." Ally laughed a little.

"Still, he may be a little difficult, but he's not

a murderer, Ally." Amelia met her eyes. "You know that, don't you?"

Ally realized she was on the spot. Amelia was there to find out if Ally had provided the detectives with any evidence against Brent.

"I wouldn't think so, Amelia. I really wouldn't." She frowned. "I'm sorry you and your family are going through this."

"Me too. I thought maybe we were finally done with law enforcement being involved in our lives, but I guess that is not the case." She shook her head. "Anyway, I'll take a box of those delicious peanut butter chocolates. They're Brent's favorite. I thought it might cheer him up a bit."

"What a sweet idea." Ally began putting together a box of the chocolates.

"I really hope that Julian isn't going to let this case get out of control. It's like people are guilty until proven innocent now."

Ally was quiet as she put the lid on the box. As

much as she agreed with Amelia, she also didn't want to say too much. She didn't want to put herself or her grandmother into a bad position with the police or the people of the town.

"I hope it all gets straightened out fast, Amelia." She handed her the box. "I hope Brent will enjoy these."

Amelia nodded. She paid for the chocolates, then walked towards the door. "Thanks for your support, Ally."

The words hung in the air as the door swung shut behind Amelia. Did Brent have her support? Ally wasn't sure.

"Who was that?" Charlotte stepped out of the kitchen just in time to see Amelia disappearing out the door.

"Amelia Nissle." Ally raised an eyebrow. "Brent's little sister."

"Oh boy. What did she want?" Charlotte peered out the front window as Amelia walked past.

"She wanted Brent's favorite chocolates. She's trying to cheer him up. I guess the detectives talked to both of them this morning as well," Ally said. "She seems pretty torn up by it all."

"The whole town is." Charlotte sighed. "Let's call it a day. I don't want to hear anymore gossip about what happened to Connor."

"Good idea." Ally nodded. As Charlotte walked towards the door to turn the lock, a shadow fell across the glass. She took a slight step back. "Are you okay?" Ally rounded the front counter as the front door swung open. Luke made his way inside the shop.

"Are you closing?"

"Yes." Charlotte seemed a little flustered.

"Your hours say you're open until five." Luke pointed to the list of hours on the front door.

"Well, given what happened to Connor, we thought it might be best to close up." Charlotte glanced over at Ally. Ally paused beside her grandmother.

"Is there something we can help you with, Detective?" Ally met his eyes with a determination not to be intimidated by him.

"Actually, I brought something that belongs to you." He drew his shoulders up and looked between the two women. "Something I thought you might be missing."

Ally resisted a glare. She had a feeling that Luke was up to something.

"What is it then?" Charlotte asked. A touch of annoyance sharpened her voice.

"Your delivery van. The police are done processing it. Julian felt it should be returned to you right away." He held out the keys. "I guess that's how things are done around here."

Charlotte took the keys from him. Ally noticed her grandmother's hand tremble as she grasped the keys.

"Thank you," Charlotte said quietly.

Ally placed her hand on her grandmother's back and rubbed a slow circle. She knew that it had to be hard for her to know that Connor had been out on a delivery for her shop when he was killed.

Luke nodded at both of them and then left the shop. Ally and Charlotte stood close to each other with the keys between them.

"I guess we better go take a look." Charlotte sighed.

"I can do it if you want, Mee-Maw." Ally looked at her grandmother with sympathy.

"No, it's okay. I should be there, too."

The two women walked out through the front door and around to the side parking lot. The small delivery van looked stoic framed by the empty asphalt.

"It's unsettling isn't it?" Charlotte stared at the van.

"Yes," Ally agreed. She knew that it had to be even more troubling to her grandmother who was used to seeing Connor driving the van.

"I keep thinking there had to be some kind of

mistake," Charlotte said. "You know I've faced a lot of loss in my life, but it never makes sense to me."

"I guess it's the one thing that never will make sense." Ally walked towards the van. "I'll take a look inside. Maybe the flowers and chocolates are still in there."

"Oh dear, the delivery. I never really thought about that. Thanks Ally." Charlotte stepped back beneath the awning of the side entrance. Ally walked to the front of the van and took a look inside the driver's side window. The window was still rolled down. She thought that was a little odd. Most people were careful enough to roll up a window when they were going to be away from a vehicle for some time. Not only that but the van had air conditioning, so it wasn't really necessary for Connor to have it rolled down, but maybe he just wanted some fresh, country air. It occurred to her that perhaps the police had rolled it down during their inspection of the vehicle.

Ally opened the driver's side door. There was

nothing out of the ordinary about the interior. Ally did notice there was some dirt beneath the pedals, but that was to be expected since so many of the driveways were still unpaved in the town. Hanging from the rearview mirror was a tiny rabbit's foot. Ally smiled at the sight of it. She had given it to her grandmother as a gift when she was a young girl. She had hoped that it would bring her grandmother luck. Her smile faded as she realized that had not turned out to be the case at all. She ducked her head back out of the front of the van and closed the door. Charlotte watched as she walked around to the back of the van.

Ally opened up the two heavy doors and looked inside. As she did she smelled the sweet scents of flowers and chocolates. The refrigerated cargo area of the van was completely empty.

"It's not here, Mee-Maw. He must have already made the delivery."

"We don't know that for sure." Charlotte walked over to her. "Maybe whoever hurt Connor took the flowers and chocolates, too."

"Why would they bother to do that?"

"Maybe just to cover their tracks in some way. Or maybe they were hungry." Charlotte peered inside. "It looks clean as a whistle in here."

"Is that unusual?" Ally asked.

"Not really. I make sure that Connor cleans the van each night since we transport food in it."

Ally thought about the dirt she had seen in the front seat. If Connor had climbed into the back to get the gift basket to deliver it, wouldn't he have tracked some of that dirt into the cargo area? Maybe he had left the basket close to the doors so he didn't have to climb in? She swept a fingertip along the floor of the van. There was not a trace of dust or dirt on it.

"I think you might be right, Mee-Maw, maybe he didn't deliver the basket after all. We should find out for sure."

"I have some of the chocolate roses left so we can put together another basket with a few other chocolates and some of the flowers in the shop and we can take it over. Just in case the first was not delivered." Charlotte headed for the door of the shop. Ally lingered beside the van. She wished there was a way to know for sure what had happened to Connor. One thing that really worried her was that Luke and Julian wouldn't investigate the crime the way they should. Luke didn't have any personal ties to the town or to Connor. Julian's mind was already set on the idea that Brent was responsible. However, Ally had a feeling that there was something much more to the crime than a case of a simple feud.

Chapter Seven

Once the gift basket was ready they loaded it into Ally's car. It felt too strange to take the van just yet and the weather was quite cool so the flowers and chocolates would stay fresh without being refrigerated. As Ally drove through Blue River towards the house of the family that had placed the order she noticed that the sidewalks were surprisingly bare.

"Where is everyone?"

"Likely filling up the bingo hall." Charlotte looked out the window. "Everyone wants to know what's happened. The bingo hall is the place to go to find out."

Ally and Charlotte spent the rest of the drive to Mainbry discussing new chocolate flavor combinations that they could try. Once Ally pulled into the driveway of the home in Mainbry they had decided to try a mocha and caramelized hazelnut milk chocolate. They weren't sure if it would work, but it would be fun making it. Just like most of the houses in Blue River and Mainbry, the driveway was dirt. Ally parked right beside the front door. When she and her grandmother reached the front door Charlotte raised her hand to knock, but the door was pulled open before she could.

"Charlotte, I didn't expect you to come." The red-faced woman smiled at Charlotte. Ally found her vaguely familiar, but she couldn't quite place who she was.

"Maureen, I wanted to see if you had received your order, I know you needed it to give it as a gift tonight," Charlotte explained.

"Oh, well, no we didn't." Maureen shook her head. "I didn't really expect to though, after I heard what happened to Connor, that poor boy."

"It's not exactly what you ordered, but we brought you a basket." Charlotte gestured to Ally.

Ally held up the basket.

"Oh, you two dears. You really didn't have to

do that. Come inside please, I've just put some tea on."

Charlotte and Ally moved inside the house. The front hall was narrow and crowded with small shoes. Ally could hear children running back and forth above them. Charlotte followed the woman all the way to the kitchen. Ally dawdled a little as she studied the home. It reminded her of a closet the way it was narrow and tall. She looked for any sign that Connor had been in the house.

"So, the delivery never came?" Charlotte sat down at an octagon shaped table. Ally stood near the doorway of the kitchen. The kitchen was large compared to the rest of the house, with wide windows that overlooked the backyard.

"No, I'm afraid it didn't. But this is just beautiful. Thank you so much. I'm very sorry to hear about what happened to Connor. In Blue River? It's hard to imagine." Her lips tensed. "I guess it really is going downhill around here."

"I wouldn't say that. But it is a terrible thing that has happened. I'm sure the detectives working on it will solve the case." Ally knew that Charlotte spoke with more confidence than she felt.

"Oh yes, they've already been here. I guess they got the address off the order. Julian was so sweet, but that other guy."

"Luke," Ally chimed in as she joined them at the table.

"Yes, he's a bit strange, isn't he?" She shook her head. "I remember when you and Julian would splash each other in the baby pool, Ally. Do you remember that?"

"Huh?" Ally shook her head. "No. When was that?"

"Oh, you two must have been about three. I was watching you both." She paused and lowered her eyes. "Before your mother passed, when I was still living in Blue River."

Ally was very surprised. She had no idea that she had ever been watched by this woman, or that Julian had been part of her daily life.

"No, I'm sorry I don't remember." Ally glanced over at her grandmother, who nodded.

"Oh, of course you wouldn't, you were too young. But you were quite mature for your age when it came to romance." Maureen giggled. "You were always trying to tackle Julian and kiss him."

Ally's cheeks burned with blush. "Really?"

"Yes, it was the most adorable thing." She sighed fondly. "You weren't with me for long, though. Your mother got you into a pre-K program and off you went."

"Thanks for sharing that with me." Ally smiled. She wondered if that was why she had such a crush on Julian when she was younger. Even though she didn't actively remember playing with Julian, she must have held onto some fond feelings for him.

"Anyway, I'm sure Julian will get to the bottom of it."

"Let's hope so." Charlotte finished her cup of tea. "I'm sorry that the delivery was late."

"That's quite all right. I appreciate you bringing it." She walked Charlotte and Ally back to the door. Just as they were stepping out, she leaned close. "Be careful, you two. It's so unsettling to think that there is a murderer on the loose."

Ally looked at her with slight surprise. She honestly hadn't thought of the situation that way. What if she was right? Was it possible that whoever killed Connor would be on the hunt for another victim? Charlotte gave Ally's hand a squeeze.

"Thanks, we'll be careful." Charlotte smiled.

***

As Charlotte and Ally drove back to the shop, Ally looked over at her grandmother. "Do you think there could be someone out there just killing for fun, Mee-Maw? I mean, could there be a serial killer?"

"Of course there could be. Blue River is a little town where nothing bad ever happens, so it's the perfect setting for a horror movie." She laughed.

"But I doubt that's what happened here. I think if the police thought it was a planned out murder they would be more concerned."

"I remember that one of the detectives said that it looked like it was not premeditated. Sounded like it might have been violent."

Charlotte nodded in agreement.

Once they returned to the shop they made some heart shaped caramel centered milk chocolates for an anniversary present. Ally found the process soothing as she dipped each chocolate.

Once the chocolates were decorated and in the fridge they closed up for the day. Ally's mind drifted to thoughts about the part of her childhood she had spent with Julian. Even then she must have seen something in him that she liked.

Chapter Eight

Around lunchtime the next day Charlotte received a phone call for a special delivery. As she hung up the phone, Ally could see the strain in her face.

"It's hard to get a call for a delivery." She shook her head. "Normally I'd be right on the phone with Connor." Her voice trembled a little. "I guess I'll take it."

"No, Mee-Maw, let me do it." Ally hugged her grandmother. "I know how hard this must be on you."

"Thanks Ally." She kissed Ally on the forehead. "It is such a help to have you here."

Those words echoed through Ally's mind as she started the engine of the delivery van. She knew that her grandmother wanted her to stay, but Ally wasn't so sure it was the right choice. It felt a bit like running away or going backwards.

Ally knew just about every road in the town,

the address on the order was familiar to her, but she couldn't quite place exactly where the street was. She pulled out the GPS from the glove compartment, but before she could start entering the address she saw that she had to clear out the last destination. Ally presumed it was from the day that Connor was killed because the van had not been used since then. The address in the GPS was different from the address that they had delivered the chocolates and flowers to. The order should have gone to Marigold Lane. Connor had inputted Marietta Lane. Ally found that to be a little strange. Did Connor have another delivery? She didn't think he had. Did he go to this address for another reason? Had Connor gone to the wrong address for the delivery? The thought weighed on her mind as she drove to the address for her delivery.

It was a small house on the outskirts of town. She parked her car and walked up the porch stairs. When she got to the top of the stairs there was a group of women gathered around a table in the center of the porch. There was a pot of tea in the center of the table. As Ally walked towards them with the boxes of chocolates, she heard the whispers begin. When she paused beside the group she could hear some of what was being said.

"Should we ask her?"

"How will we ever know if we don't?"

"It seems a bit rude."

"Rude or not, she was the last person to see him."

Ally's heart sank as she realized that they wanted to find out about Connor's death.

"Here are the chocolates." She set the boxes down on the table between all of them. All of the women grew silent. Ally felt scrutinized as she avoided looking at any of them. "Okay, I'll just be going." She turned on her heel and began to walk away.

"Wait, please." One of the women stood up from the table. "I'm sorry this must seem strange to you. We're not trying to be rude, but we love murder mysteries, and we're just so excited to have one in our own town."

Ally stared at the group. "You can't be serious."

"Oh, it's not as if we're asking for the gory details, just the facts." Another woman stood up.

Ally shook her head. "This isn't a book, ladies. This is real. Connor grew up here, just like I did."

"We know it's real, we just want some information! We want to help figure out what happened to him! What's so wrong with that?" The first woman looked directly at Ally. "How could it hurt to have extra eyes on the situation?"

Ally frowned. "I'm sorry, I don't have any information. If you want to know what's happening with the case you can always check in with the police department. Otherwise, enjoy the chocolates."

This time she walked out without stopping. She felt a little angry. But more than anything she thought the women were right. Not that they should be studying Connor's death as if it were the book of the year, but that someone needed to find out the truth about what had happened to Connor.

As soon as she got back to the van she decided that she would go to the address that was plugged into the GPS. It was one place that she was almost positive the police hadn't looked. With her doubts about Luke's dedication to finding the truth, she didn't want to count on him or Julian to investigate it on their own.

As Ally drove towards the address she felt a little uneasy. As she crossed the border from Blue River to Mainbry she entered a part of Mainbry that she had never been to before or at least didn't remember going to. It never occurred to her that it even existed, probably because her grandmother kept her away from it. It wasn't a slum as she had seen in the city, it was an abandoned property with overgrown land. Nature was wild. Even the road she drove on was littered with leaves and fallen tree limbs. It was clear that someone had been driving on it however, because the limbs were pushed to the side.

Ally continued down the road towards the blip on the GPS. It was hard for her to believe that there was anything to drive towards with such barren landscape around her. Had Connor really driven this way without realizing that he was lost? Then she noticed that there wasn't really a safe way to turn around. The sides of the road were lined with ditches. Maneuvering a delivery van into a U-turn would be nearly impossible. Maybe Connor had been looking for a driveway, or maybe he had just been determined to get to the address.

"You will reach your destination in point two miles."

The ghostly voice made Ally feel even more uneasy. She wasn't sure she wanted to reach her destination. She nearly passed the driveway as it was set back from the road and covered in brush. There was an opening just wide enough to squeeze the van through. She hesitated to actually drive into it. Was it safe? She knew that she would have to get turned around somehow. Cautiously she nudged the van onto the driveway. She heard a few snaps of branches as she ran over them. Before her appeared an old building that looked like a factory. It had broken windows and crumbling brick. It was quite obviously no longer in use. However, the driveway beyond the entrance had been completely cleared. Though the grass that lined the driveway was still quite tall, it was clear that it had been cut back. Someone had taken the time to do minimal maintenance on the property.

"Maybe they're trying to sell it?" Ally drove all the way to the end of the driveway. She didn't see any other cars, or any other signs of life. The entire area had such a desolate feeling, as if a deep sadness lingered there. Ally turned off the engine and stepped out of the van. She had come this far, she thought it was worth it to take a closer look. As she stepped out of the van she noticed that there was a small, shiny puddle on the pavement of the driveway. It looked like it had dripped from the bottom of a vehicle. She studied it for a moment and then looked up at the building again.

"Were you here, Connor?"

Her voice carried louder than she expected in the emptiness. She walked up to the front of the building just to see what it might be like inside. When she peered through one of the broken windows she was confronted by a large, plastic curtain. It was black, blocking the view of anything that might be beyond it. However, it did not block the smell. It was thick and took her breath away. She couldn't quite place what it was, but she knew that she had smelled it somewhere before. She felt an urge to go inside and investigate, but she resisted. Something didn't feel right. Her heart began to pound, though she had no idea why she was afraid.

"Chill out, Ally, it's just an old building." She shook her head and walked back to the van. As she walked away from the window she thought she heard a flutter of the plastic curtain. When she turned back it was still. She shook her head again and climbed into the cab of the van. As she made her way back down the driveway she wondered who would have been out there and why. She decided that she would find out what she could about the property. Maybe that would put her mind at ease. She knew that there was a good chance that Connor had not been there at all. He might have realized the address was wrong before he ever reached the old factory. Still, she thought it was worth looking into.

***

Ally drove back to the shop with thoughts of the dilapidated building weighing on her mind. She wanted to put it out of her head, but every time she tried to treat it as nothing to be concerned about, it would pop back up. Had Connor been there? She wished there was a way she could know for sure. In order to put her mind at ease she knew that she was going to have to find out more about the building. When she arrived at the shop, her grandmother was standing outside talking to another woman. It took Ally a moment but she recognized the woman as an old teacher of hers, Gina Kiery.

"Ally!" Gina smiled at her as she stepped out of the van. "I was just talking about you."

"Me?" Ally looked between the two women. "Why?"

"Well, you were one of my favorite students. I'm glad to see you back home."

"I'm just visiting, but thank you." It meant a lot to Ally that she would consider her to be a favorite student.

"Your grandmother was telling me how you're single now." Gina winked at Ally. "I guess that won't be true for long since Brent is single, too."

Just then she remembered that Gina was her teacher when she was briefly dating Brent. She tried to hide a blush as she remembered the teacher once catching the two of them behind the building. They were just sharing playful kisses, but it was still an embarrassing moment.

"I don't know about that. I'm sure Brent has moved on." Ally smiled politely. "I'm really just here to help in the shop."

"Of course you are. Especially after what happened to poor Connor. He was such a good, young man. This town has lost a real gem."

Ally nodded. She could agree with that. What she didn't know, was why. It seemed so impossible to her for someone to be murdered for no reason at all. She knew that it happened all of the time, every day in fact, but not in her little town, and not to someone she knew.

"Gina was just telling me about the plans for Connor's service." Charlotte tilted her head towards the shop. "Why don't we all go inside?"

"Oh, I would love to but I can't. I have to get to the florist and make sure the flowers are lined up for the service. I've been trying to help out Marla. It's just such a shame. Connor was her only child you know." She sighed. "It's good you're here, Ally." She smiled at Ally once more and then walked away.

"That delivery took longer than I thought it would." Charlotte held open the door to the shop. "Did everything go okay?"

"Yes, I'm sorry. I got caught up." Ally paused a moment. She thought about telling her grandmother about the address and the factory. But she didn't want to upset her more than she already was. Ally really didn't know that much anyway.

"Caught up, how?" Charlotte pressed as the two headed for the kitchen.

"Oh, just turned around." Ally floundered for an explanation. She wasn't accustomed to lying to her grandmother.

"Listen to me, Ally, I want the truth. What took so long?" Charlotte turned to face her granddaughter. Ally realized that she was not going to successfully lie to her grandmother.

"I found another address in the GPS. It looked like Connor might have put in the wrong address when he went to make the delivery or went to that address for some other reason. So I decided to go check it out."

"And?" Charlotte looked at her anxiously.

"And I found an old abandoned building. It looked like a factory. But it looked like someone might have been using it recently. It is on Marietta Lane. I never even knew it existed. Did you?" Ally looked at her grandmother curiously.

Charlotte started to shake her head and then she took a sharp breath. "Oh yes, I remember now. I can't believe that it is still standing. It was built when you were little. A wealthy man was going to use Mainbry for a manufacturing hub. The locals were pretty excited about the job creation. But something went wrong and he never even opened the factory. As far as I know nothing was ever moved in. I just assumed that it had been bulldozed a long time ago."

"Do you remember who owned it?"

"No. I'm not sure. I can make some phone calls and find out though. In the meantime, you should talk to Julian." Charlotte met Ally's eyes. "This is information they should have. If Connor went to the factory by mistake or even on purpose it might be a missing link in their investigation."

"But I don't even know for sure that he was there." Ally frowned. "I mean, Connor probably figured out that he was going in the wrong direction and turned around."

"What if he didn't?" Charlotte pressed. "This is not the time to withhold information from the police, Ally. I really think that you need to go tell Julian as soon as possible."

"All right," Ally reluctantly agreed. She didn't really want to risk running into Luke, but she knew her grandmother was right. Maybe this would inspire the detectives to think outside the box a little when it came to Connor's death.

"Don't worry about the shop, I'll close it up. I'll see you at home, okay?" Charlotte smiled at her. "Don't let Luke get to you. Julian will listen to you."

Ally nodded as if she believed her grandmother, but she had a nagging feeling that she was wrong. Luke seemed to be close enough to have a good hold on Julian. Ally wasn't sure that she would be able to break through that influence.

Chapter Nine

Ally quickly ate a piece of chocolate cake. Her grandmother had made it and it was so moist and delicious without being too sweet that she had to stop herself from having another piece. After promising herself that she would make an effort to eat healthier in future as she could not have a diet that consisted mainly of chocolate while she was in Blue River, even though she wanted it to, she headed to the police station. She enjoyed the walk there. The fresh, crisp air helped clear her mind.

The local police station was a small building. It had several large desks in one room. The remainder of the station had a few holding cells. Ally knew this because her high school would always do a tour of the police station prior to big sports events and dances. It was meant to be a reminder of the consequences of their choices. Ally pulled open the door and was greeted by the strong scent of cinnamon. She was so distracted by the smell that she didn't notice Luke at first. He stood a few feet from the door.

"Ally?"

Ally looked over at him with surprise. For the first time she didn't just notice how handsome he was, she felt a jolt of attraction. It wasn't anything she expected. She hadn't been attracted to anyone since her divorce. Certainly not to Luke, who had gone out of his way to suspect and question her.

"I'm looking for Julian."

Luke swept his eyes over her for a moment. Then he tilted his head towards the desks. "He's out at the moment. Is there something I can help you with?"

Ally fought the urge to turn around and walk out of the police station. She didn't want to discuss anything with Luke.

"Maybe I'll just come back when Julian is here."

"Wait." Luke settled his eyes on hers. "Is it about the case?"

"I think I should talk to Julian." Ally felt her stubbornness billow within her.

"That doesn't really answer the question." Luke managed to edge his way between her and the door. "If you have some information that pertains to the case there's no reason to withhold it. I can pass it on to Julian."

"I'm not withholding anything." Ally took a step further into the police station in order to create some distance between them. "I just would prefer to speak to Julian."

Luke's brows knitted as if he was about to attempt to force her, but then his expression relaxed. "He'll be back in a minute or two. Do you want to wait?"

Ally didn't want to wait. She didn't want to spend a second more around Luke. But she also didn't want to leave without telling someone about what she had found. It could be important.

"He'll be back soon?" She tried to ignore the way his very distracting eyes were attempting to bore into hers.

"Yes. And I promise not to bite." He smiled. The expression was disturbing to Ally, who expected quite the opposite from Luke. She wasn't sure if he was making fun of her or trying to reassure her.

"All right, I'll wait." Ally stepped past him towards the nearest open chair. Luke followed after her. As he sat down across the desk from her, Ally watched him.

"I'd rather just wait by myself," Ally muttered.

"Well, this is my desk." Luke smiled at her again. When he smiled a small dimple was revealed in the slope of his cheek. Despite her better judgment Ally felt that jolt of attraction again. It startled her and she was a little disappointed in herself for feeling it. "But I can find something else to do." Luke frowned. Ally guessed that he had been able to read the disappointment on her face. She didn't ask him to stay. Luke walked away from the desks and through the door that led to the holding cells.

Ally sat perfectly still for a few moments. She

noticed that the remaining staff were spaced quite far from her. She was feeling a bit anxious waiting for Julian so she decided to walk around a bit and try to calm her nerves. She started pacing back and forth. She walked behind Luke's desk and looked down to avoid a trashcan. What she saw on the top of the trashcan made her chest tighten and her blood run cold. It was a pink ribbon. The exact shade of pink that had been on the box of chocolates that Connor was to deliver the day he died. The same box of chocolates that had gone missing.

Her heart pounded against her chest, making her chest feel even worse. Had they found the chocolates? Or had Luke decided to dispose of some evidence? She stared hard at the ribbon. It crossed her mind to pluck it out and confront him with it. But she decided against it. If Luke was smart enough to get away with murder then he wasn't going to be taken down by just anyone. She had to make sure that she had all of the evidence she needed before she could confront him. She saw the door to the holding cell begin to swing open. Luke was the last person that she wanted to see. She picked up her purse off her chair and walked towards the door. She reached it just as Julian was pulling it open.

"Ally? What are you doing here?" Julian offered her a radiant smile. Ally was too nervous to even notice.

"Nothing. False alarm," she mumbled as she walked past him. Julian caught her lightly by the inside of her elbow.

"Ally, are you okay?" He searched her eyes. "Did something happen that I should know about?"

Ally hesitated. She wondered if she should go ahead and tell him about the factory. However, she knew that she couldn't. Not if Luke was involved. She knew that Julian could be trusted, but that didn't mean that he wouldn't let information slip to his partner. She felt Julian's eyes on her as he released her elbow.

"You can always talk to me, Ally," he spoke in

a confidential tone. "If there's something you need to get off your chest."

Ally stepped through the door and cast a brief smile over her shoulder. She was afraid that if she lingered a moment longer she would spill her entire life story to Julian so she could unburden herself and make it someone else's problem.

Ally tried to shake off the entire experience, but she felt more confused than ever as she walked back towards the shop. In many ways she had expected Julian to solve all of her problems. She would tell him about the factory, he would check it out, and Connor's killer would be discovered. But seeing that ribbon had thrown everything off for her. Why did Luke have it? Why did he throw it away if it was evidence? He had voiced his accusations against her and her grandmother to Julian. He had also accused Brent. Was that an attempt to deflect guilt? She was worried as she walked. If Luke could eliminate Connor, he could eliminate Julian as well. Ally decided she would have to be extra careful about what she told Julian, or she might put him at great risk.

***

Ally had every intention of rushing right into her grandmother's shop and telling her what she had seen. However, when she arrived she spotted Julian standing in front of the counter. She assumed he must have driven from the police station while she walked. He leaned casually with one elbow against the counter as he talked with Charlotte. Ally felt her heart lurch. This was her chance. Julian was alone, without Luke to listen in on what she had to say. She opened the door to the shop and stepped inside. Julian turned at the sound of the bell over the door.

"Ally, just who I hoped to see." He smiled at her. Ally wanted to smile in return but she couldn't bring herself to. Her mind filled with memories of just how charming Julian had always been. He was one of the most popular students in school. He was voted likely to be most successful. He had a way of getting everyone to believe in him and to want to be near him. He was one of those people that commanded your attention and didn't mind basking in it. Could he really be completely ignorant about Luke being involved in the crime? Ally's teeth clenched at the very thought. She hated to suspect Julian, but how could he work one on one with Luke on the case and not see that Luke was up to something?

"Oh?" She cleared her throat.

"Yes. Luke told me that you came to the police station specifically to speak to me, and then you just disappeared. I wanted to make sure that you were okay and see what you needed. It seemed like you were in a rush to leave." He straightened up and walked towards her. "What's going on? Did something happen? Did you find out something about Connor's murder?"

"Uh, no not really." Ally felt her heart beat in her throat. She could barely get her words past the thumping.

"So, you went to the police station and asked for me for no reason?" Julian raised an eyebrow.

"That seems rather odd to me."

"Well, I..." Ally met her grandmother's eyes. Charlotte gave a questioning look. "I thought I had some information, but then I realized that it probably wasn't that important."

"Any information is important. What was it about?" Julian stepped to the side. Ally couldn't be sure if he was intentionally blocking her grandmother from view, but the movement did just that. He met her eyes with a hardness that she hadn't noticed before. "Murder is a serious crime, Ally. Anything you may know is important."

"I know that." Ally fought off a little dizziness and panic. She attempted to make something up. "It's just that I didn't think that Brent and Connor were actively fighting. I thought you should know that. But then I realized that my information wasn't very reliable. So, I decided to just leave. It's nothing really."

Julian's silence spoke louder than anything he could say. Ally suspected that he did not believe her. She tightened her lips and did her best to appear casual.

"Ally, I just want you to know that you can come to me, with anything that you might be concerned about. Okay?" He reached out and took her hand. Ally tried to stop the excitement that rushed through her like a tidal wave. Julian was holding her hand. Julian, who when she was growing up she once thought she would give anything to marry. Ally took a deep breath and smiled.

"I know that, Julian. There's nothing to be concerned about with such a great detective on the case."

"Now, that's what I like to hear." Julian laughed and let go of her hand. He started to walk out of the shop, then paused at the door. He looked back at her with interest. "We should get together sometime. To catch up."

Ally could only nod in return. There was absolutely no reason for them to catch up. They had never really had any history. She had just had a silly childhood crush. After hearing about the time they spent in a kiddie pool together though, maybe they did have some connection. Maybe Julian would be the distraction that she needed to get over her divorce. After the case was solved.

Once Julian left, Ally turned towards her grandmother.

"Ally, what was all of that about?" Charlotte frowned. She walked around the counter towards her. "Is everything okay?"

Ally opened her mouth to tell her grandmother the truth, but again she hesitated. Not because she didn't want to tell her grandmother, but she worried about her. If Luke really was involved in Connor's murder, how far would he go to cover that up? Charlotte tended to say pretty much whatever she pleased at any given time, which put her at risk of confronting Luke. Ally didn't want to go after Luke just yet. She wanted to gather more evidence against him first. She also wanted to find out if Julian knew about Luke's involvement. Maybe he did and he was just waiting for proof to arrest him.

"Honestly, I decided not to tell them about the old factory. I don't think it really matters. I'm sure they checked the GPS during their investigation. Besides, the place is completely empty." Ally shook her head. "Connor's funeral is tomorrow, and I just want to focus on that."

"You're right, Ally. His mother will need our support. Still, I think you should have mentioned the factory to Julian. Maybe next time you see him?"

"Maybe." Ally nodded. "Do you need any help with anything?"

"Sure, I'm decorating a batch of chocolates to take to the service tomorrow. Would you like to help?" Charlotte studied her with a worried frown. Ally could tell that her grandmother didn't completely believe what she said.

"Absolutely."

Ally followed her grandmother into the kitchen. She rarely lied to her, but this time, she felt it was for the best.

Chapter Ten

Ally woke up the next morning with a sick feeling in the pit of her stomach. Up until today she had been in denial of Connor's death. But today was the funeral. She wouldn't be able to hide from it anymore. She knew that even though she and Connor had never been terribly close they shared something just by growing up together in the same town. More than that, she had possibly been the last person that Connor had spoken to. She kept replaying in her mind what she had said and whether she had been kind. She knew that it was a losing battle to try to figure it out, but she still tried.

For the funeral she selected a simple black dress. She tied her brown hair back in a tight, straight braid. When she stepped out into the living room her grandmother was already waiting. She also wore a black dress, and had swept back her hair.

"Are you ready for this?"

"I think so." Ally straightened her dress. "As ready as I can be."

"True. I don't think any of us are really ready for it." Charlotte reached out and brushed Ally's hair back from her forehead. "The important thing now is that we are strong for Connor's mother."

Ally nodded. She could see the immense compassion in her grandmother's deep-green eyes. Charlotte knew what it was like to lose a child. As they walked towards the church they were surrounded by what appeared to be every other person in town, dressed in dark clothing and wearing solemn expressions. No one waved or spoke to one another. It was as if everyone had gotten together and agreed that this was one day they should be silent. When they reached the church, organ music drifted from its windows. Ally shivered at the memory of the melancholic sound.

She found it hard to step into the church. As a young girl she had gone on occasion with friends, but it had always seemed like a somber place to her. She had been to more funerals there than church services. Most of the faces around her were people she had known or was at least familiar with since she was a child. It was surreal to be back in a place where she had said goodbye to her mother. As she waited for the service to begin she lingered near the front door. She could hear snippets of hushed conversation.

"It's just so sad that this happened."

"I'm not sure if we're ever going to be the same."

"I don't understand why this town is changing. Murder? Here?"

"Maybe if Connor hadn't caused such a commotion over that bar fight with Brent he would still be alive."

That comment made Ally look up with surprise. The man who said it was at least forty years her senior. She remembered him as a grouchy man around town. He would sit on his porch and holler at the kids playing in the street if he thought they were being too loud. He looked just as grouchy now. Curious, she listened more closely to his conversation with a man she did not recognize.

"Surely a bar fight didn't lead to this." The other man shook his head.

"Listen, these are young men. They're both troublemakers really. They do impulsive things. Brent probably wanted to get revenge for the way that he was treated. Connor made a fool of him that night."

"Was it recent?"

"No, it was at least a year ago."

The other man huffed. "That's ridiculous, who would hold a grudge that long?"

"The problems between those two families go back generations. I'm sure it wasn't just about one drunken bar fight. That was probably just the icing on the cake."

"I don't know, it's hard to believe."

"That's what everyone's saying around town.

It was Brent that did it. No one is even thinking about another suspect." The grumpy man shrugged. "It was bound to happen eventually."

"William, for God's sake have some respect." A woman grabbed onto William's arm. "We're here to honor the dead, not gossip."

"Sorry Mavis, I'm just being honest." He shrugged again. She led him away in an effort to silence him. Ally shifted uncomfortably from one foot to the other. She didn't like how quickly the whole town was pinning the murder on Brent. She wasn't certain anymore that he had nothing to do with it. If so many people suspected him, maybe they were right? Was she just blinded by her memories of an innocent boy who had been her first boyfriend and good friend? She obviously didn't have the best judgment when it came to the people she gave her heart to.

"Are you doing okay, Ally?" Charlotte placed her hand lightly on Ally's shoulder. She had just broken away from a crowd of ladies about her age. Ally noticed a misting in her grandmother's eyes.

She remembered that she was not the only one who had said goodbye to her mother.

"Yes. It's just a sad day." She hugged her grandmother.

"That it is. Why don't we sit down?" Charlotte gestured to one of the pews. Ally followed after her. Soon everyone in the church was taking their seats. Ally settled in for the service. As expected many people from the community spoke about Connor's influence on them. Members of Connor's family also stood up and said a few words. Connor's mother read a poem that she had read to Connor as part of a bedtime ritual. Ally's eyes were red and swollen by the time the service shifted to the more traditional process. During this shift, the front door of the church swung open. Light spilled into the comparatively dim environment. Framed in that light was Brent Nissle.

A collective gasp silenced the church before avid whispering began. Brent stood awkwardly at the back of the pews. Connor's mother stared at him as he slowly walked towards the casket.

"Oh dear, this isn't going to be good." Charlotte squeezed Ally's hand.

"Please, I just want to pay my respects," Brent spoke in a mild tone. He paused a few feet away from the casket as if seeking permission. Connor's mother stood up and glared at him.

"How dare you show your face here, on the day I lay my son to rest. The son that you took from me," her voice shook with rage.

"I didn't," Brent stammered. "I didn't do it. Connor and I had our problems, I won't lie, but I would never do this. You have to believe that."

"I don't have to believe anything." She shook her head. "I want you to leave. Right now."

"All right, all right I will. I didn't mean to cause you any more pain. I swear I didn't." As Brent turned to walk out of the church, the entrance doors swung open. To Ally's surprise, Julian and Luke walked in. From their stern strides and tight expressions she had a feeling they were there for more than just the funeral. They waited until Brent reached the back of the pews. Ally stood up.

"Ally, where are you going?" Charlotte whispered.

"I want to talk to Brent," Ally whispered back.

"Don't you think this isn't the right time for that?" Charlotte frowned. "It's rather disrespectful."

Ally heard her grandmother's words, but she pretended that she didn't. She saw Julian step closer to Brent. The two began to exchange words. Ally hurried down the aisle to reach them. She wanted to know what they were talking about. When she got close enough she heard Luke step in and begin speaking as well.

"It's either going to happen here, or outside. If you have any decency you'll come outside without a scene."

Ally's heart skipped a beat. Brent hung his head. His voice was muffled, "All right. Let's go."

Luke and Julian flanked Brent. The three men walked out the door. Ally followed after them. As soon as they were outside, Luke grabbed Brent's arm and spun him around so that he could grab the other arm as well.

"What are you doing?" Ally blurted out.

Luke and Julian both turned to look at her. Luke finished handcuffing Brent while Julian walked over to Ally.

"We're arresting Brent. We just got the arrest warrant," Julian explained.

"Easy!" Brent barked at Luke who tightened the handcuffs.

"Isn't that a little hasty?" Ally frowned. She looked at Luke with disapproval as he ignored Brent's complaints.

Luke smiled at Ally and said in a condescending tone, "Don't worry about it, Ally. We'll do the police work, you make chocolates."

Ally scowled at him. "I don't see how you can be arresting him without evidence."

"Who says we don't have evidence?" Luke asked. She was surprised that he still had his attention focused on her. "Is there something you know that we should know, Ally?"

"No," she muttered. "Nothing at all."

Brent turned around to look at Ally, though Luke held tightly to his arm. Brent looked into her eyes. Her heart melted as he looked fourteen all over again. She remembered their brief romance and their friendship.

"Ally, I didn't do this. I didn't."

"She's not the one you have to convince." Luke steered him passed Ally towards his car. As the two walked passed her Ally caught a whiff of something slightly sweet. She presumed it was one of their aftershaves.

Ally's heart ached as she watched Brent go. Could he have really changed into a murderer? She didn't want to believe that he could.

"Julian, don't you think you could be wrong?" Ally looked at Julian with concern.

"No Ally. I don't. A murderer will do anything to convince you that he's innocent. Just let us handle it." Ally took a step back. The look in Julian's eyes was so determined that Ally was stunned by it. She knew then that there was no changing his mind. As far as Julian was concerned, Brent was guilty.

Chapter Eleven

Ally made her way back into the church as quietly as possible. She knew that the people inside were only trying to pay their respects. However, the way most were gossiping about Brent made her uneasy. She knew that justice in small towns could sometimes be more of a popularity contest than the result of a thorough investigation. When she sat back down beside her grandmother, she felt the warmth of her grandmother's hand press lightly on her hand. Ally appreciated the reassurance.

The remainder of the service was uninterrupted and as solemn as expected. By the time the service reached its conclusion Ally had tears in her eyes. She was sad for Connor and his family, but she was also sad for Brent. She couldn't believe that he could have done this and she believed that he was being accused of a crime that he did not commit. After saying a polite goodbye to Connor's mother, Ally and her grandmother began the walk back to the cottage. Ally was quiet as she listened to the subtle noises of the town.

"What's going on in that head of yours, Ally?" Charlotte asked.

"Do you know they arrested Brent?" Ally grimaced.

"Oh, they did?" Charlotte's eyes widened. "I thought they just took him outside to prevent a commotion. I guess they must have some pretty good evidence against him."

"That's just the thing. I don't think they do." Ally narrowed her eyes. "How can they? I mean what evidence is there other than Connor's body being dumped right by Brent's shop?"

"Maybe they have more evidence than we know of and there is their history of conflict." Charlotte looked over at her grimly. "It is pretty odd that Connor's body was left near Brent's business."

"It is odd." Ally sighed. "Because why would

anyone murder someone and then dump their body right next to their own shop?"

"Well, maybe he panicked and wanted to get rid of it as quickly as he could. If that's the case then he might have thought leaving it where he did was his only option. I mean, most rational, logical people don't kill people, Ally, so you can't expect them to think with a clear mind." She paused beside the florist. "I'm going to get some flowers. Do you want to come inside with me?"

"No, I'll stay out here."

"Okay, I'll just be a minute."

Once Charlotte had disappeared into the shop, Ally turned to watch the other residents walking back to their homes. She studied each one. If it wasn't Brent that had killed Connor, could it have been someone who attended the funeral? She wished she had paid more attention when Brent walked into the church. The reactions of the other people there might have given her a clue as to who might be involved in Connor's death.

"Ally!"

Ally nearly jumped out of her skin. Her grandmother frowned and handed her some flowers to carry.

"This has really gotten under your skin, hasn't it? Why are you so sure that Brent didn't do it?"

"Because he told me he didn't." Ally fell into step with her grandmother.

"What do you mean?"

"I mean when he was being arrested, he looked me in the eyes and told me he didn't do it." Ally pursed her lips.

"Ally, of course he said he didn't do it, that doesn't mean that he didn't."

"Mee-Maw, I know Brent. He has never been able to lie to me. I've always been able to tell. I could tell that he wasn't lying when he said that to me," Ally stated confidently. "There is no doubt in my mind."

"Ally, that was over ten years ago. Just because you could tell back then, doesn't mean that Brent hasn't changed and didn't learn to become a better liar. Why would Julian and Luke arrest him if they didn't believe he did it?" She gave Ally a soft hug from the side. "I think you're a little too close to this situation. You're already dealing with so many emotions about your marriage and now you've come home to deal with this."

"Mee-Maw, I'm not being overly emotional. I know what I know." Ally crossed her arms stubbornly.

Charlotte raised an eyebrow. "Now that's a look I recall. Fine, to tell you the truth, I'm not convinced it was Brent either. But that still doesn't explain why Julian and Luke arrested him. They must have something on him."

"Or they just want to wrap up the case fast enough to be able to go fishing next weekend." Ally drew her lips into a stern line indicating her displeasure.

"Ally, I don't know much about Luke, but I'd say that Julian has higher standards than that.

Just because this is a small town, that doesn't mean that the police detectives don't do their job." She paused outside the cottage. "I have to take Arnold for a walk. Do you want to join us?"

"No, I think I'll just rest for a while," Ally replied. "Maybe a nap will clear my head."

"Try not to get too wrapped up in it, Ally. You have a kind heart, but none of this is yours to get stressed about. You have enough weighing on your mind."

Charlotte gave Ally's shoulder a light pat. Then she headed off to find Arnold's leash. At her grandmother's words Ally was reminded of the reason she had come to Blue River in the first place. She wanted to recover from the heartbreak of a divorce. Perhaps her grandmother was right and she was using Connor's death as a way to avoid confronting the pain of her separation from her husband. Even if she was right though, Ally couldn't shake the need to find out the truth.

**

When Ally stepped into her room Peaches

jumped down from the bed to greet her with a warm nuzzle and purr. Ally felt a sense of relief at the sight of the cat. She scooped her up and carried her over to the bed.

"What a rough day, Peaches." She sat down on the edge of the bed and Peaches settled right into her lap. "Sometimes I think that no one is interested in the truth anymore." She shook her head. "Luke is involved in this, I know he is. I just hope Julian isn't, too." As the cat purred, Ally felt her body begin to relax. She could feel the stress leaving her.

When things had begun getting tense between her and Daniel, spending time with Peaches had been the only thing that kept her calm. Although she had friends she could have called, Peaches kept all of her secrets. She never had to worry about the cat judging her or convincing her that her intuition was wrong. Again her feline friend was serving as her solace in the middle of the unfolding chaos.

Ally found it hard to believe that anyone could

survive life without a pet of some kind. Maybe she wouldn't find snuggling up to Arnold as relaxing as cuddling with Peaches, but she knew that her grandmother loved that little pig just as much. It made her mind shift back to Julian. She wondered if he had a pet. It was funny to her how it only took seeing an old crush to spin around her decision that she would never love again. Now Julian was creeping into her mind without her permission. She found herself imagining what it would be like to go out with him like he had suggested.

"Before any of that can happen, Connor's murder has to be solved."

When she was finally able to drift off to sleep, Ally's dreams were strange. A mixture of faces, a mixture of locations, as her past, her present, and her future all attempted to blend into one. In the middle of the night she woke up with a start. As she stared into the darkness she knew what she had to do. She couldn't just let her suspicions linger, she had to find out the truth.

Chapter Twelve

It wasn't often that Ally woke before her grandmother. She could count on one hand the amount of times she'd known her grandmother to sleep past six. Ally made sure she was awake by five. She dressed as quietly as she could. She stopped long enough to put out food for Peaches and to leave behind a note saying she was going out for a few hours.

As soon as she set off she felt a fluttering in her stomach. She munched on one of the triple chocolate muffins she had made. They were not too bad. She was sure that they would have been better if her grandmother had been the one to make them. But there was still something so satisfying about eating something that she had baked herself.

The drive towards the old factory was a quiet one. There were very few other cars on the road. Ally noticed a police patrol car making its rounds, but other than that she was alone. She was determined to get a closer look at the factory in the hope of figuring out just what was happening there. By the time she reached the long driveway, her muffin was gone and her stomach was still fluttering. It wasn't hunger, it was nerves. Would Luke be there waiting for her? Had Julian reported back to him that she was acting strange? She shook off the idea. She didn't want to think of Julian and Luke being so close. But until she knew for sure that they weren't, she had to be cautious.

Ally drove around behind the factory to park her car so that it could not be seen from the road. The grass was very wild behind the building. Structures that had likely once been intended for extra storage were in different states of crumbling. Ally shook her head at the waste. Why would someone buy the property just to neglect it?

Cautiously, she opened her car door and stepped out. The morning sun was already hot as it beat down on the aging factory. Ally surveyed the outside of the building. Although it was unkempt and overgrown there were signs that someone had been there. The grass by the doors was trampled down. There was a scrape in the dirt where the door had been opened and closed. Ally didn't find any footprints. She suspected that might mean that whoever had been in the factory did not want anyone to know. She looked at the door for a long moment. She knew that once she chose to open it and enter the building she was technically breaking the law. However, with Brent being arrested for something she was sure that he didn't do, and Luke probably having Julian's ear, Ally felt as if she had no choice but to go inside.

Ally opened the door and was immediately confronted with a strange smell. She couldn't quite place what it was. With some hesitation she stuck her head inside the factory and looked around. There were enough high windows to allow the natural light from outside in. Ally could see dust was illuminated in the air by beams of sunlight. However, there was a large, long metal table in the middle of the wide open space. It looked shiny, as if someone had just wiped it down. Ally stepped all of the way inside the factory. It didn't appear that anyone else was there.

As she walked towards the table her heart raced with every footstep. She was going down a potentially dangerous path and had no idea where it was going to lead. When she paused beside the table she noticed that there wasn't a speck of dust on it. Someone went to a lot of trouble to make sure it was clean while the rest of the factory appeared to be untouched. There were a few lockers lined up against a wall where workers were meant to store their personal items. Workers that had never been hired, as the factory had never even opened.

Despite the fact that no one had ever actively worked in the factory, Ally had an eerie sensation along the back of her neck, as if the factory was filled with invisible eyes watching her. She looked over her shoulder towards the door. It was still open about an inch or so. It was clear that no one cared to lock the door, or chain anything up, so it was not likely that anything valuable was stored inside. Still, why would this one table be kept so clean? Why would it be such a secret that activity was occurring inside the factory? What was that smell?

Ally ducked down to look under the table. As she did, she heard a voice. It made her entire body tighten up with every muscle frozen. She listened closely to it. Ally didn't recognize the voice and couldn't quite make out the words, but she could tell that it was getting closer. Her throat went dry with anxiety as she wondered if she would be caught inside the factory. If she was caught who would catch her?

Ally moved away from the table and looked for a place to hide. Most of the factory was wide open, aside from the lockers. They didn't offer much place to hide either, because they were flush against the wall. She knew that she only had one choice. She ran over to the lockers and jerked the first one in the line open. Luckily it was open from top to bottom with a hook in the back. It was wider than conventional lockers, probably for tool storage. She climbed inside. The cool metal touched her elbows and pressed against the top of her head. It felt very claustrophobic. She gulped as she pulled the door shut. A subtle click let her know that the door was shut all the way. What she didn't know was whether it was locked. She tucked herself away just in time as the person who she had heard, swung the factory door open all the way.

"Why is this door open?" A second voice barked. Ally couldn't see who had walked in. But she didn't recognize either of the voices.

"I don't know. It's usually closed, but we don't keep it locked."

"Why not?" the other voice demanded. "Do you want to get caught?"

"No, what I want is to keep things as inconspicuous as possible. If you put a shiny padlock on an old, abandoned factory you're asking for attention. Besides the stuff is never stored here very long."

"That's a good point, I guess. It just makes me nervous. This is quality product."

"Let's take a look."

Ally could hear footsteps drawing closer. She took as shallow breaths as she could manage. She clenched her teeth in an attempt to hold back her fear.

"I don't know what you're thinking questioning my product. I've never been anything but honest and often quite generous."

"Enough with the sales pitch, let me see what you have there."

Ally's heart was in her throat. Was it drugs? Diamonds? It could have been anything at all.

She heard something strike the table. Then the two men mumbled to each other.

"Is that all of it?"

"It's all he ordered."

"Well, it looks a little slim."

"It's not slim at all. Let's count it."

"Oh trust me, we'll be counting it."

"No need to get hostile."

"I'm not hostile, but I won't be jerked around either. He ordered a certain amount of product and it better be here. We have customers waiting."

"All right, all right. Let's get to it."

Ally closed her eyes. Her fear spiked as sharp pain pounded in her head. What had she gotten herself into? If the men found her in the locker she would surely end up just like Connor. Was Connor somehow involved with these men? Or did he walk in on something that got him killed? She had just done the same thing. She listened closely just in case she lived long enough to relay what she heard to Julian. She could have kicked herself for not telling him the truth and having him there with her, or even better, instead of her. She could have told him everything now, if she wasn't locked up in a tiny locker.

"This is premium."

"It looks good."

Ally was hit with another cloud of the scent she had breathed in when she opened the door. It was more potent this time. The smell was vaguely familiar to her, but she couldn't place it. What was it? Was it aftershave? Was it some kind of drug? She tried to remain focused on what the men were saying outside.

"It is the best."

"It stinks though."

"That will wear off by the time you box and ship it. It just means it's fresh. So you see, it's all there, I didn't cheat you."

"Good, let me put it away then I'll get you your money." Ally heard a scraping noise. Then she heard footsteps headed in her direction. She bit into her bottom lip to keep from crying out as the footsteps got closer and closer to where she was hiding.

"Wait just a minute. Money first."

"Fine, whatever. It's in the trunk, come out

with me."

"Gladly."

She heard the two men walking back towards the door. Her heart raced. This was her chance. She knew it might be her only chance. As soon as she heard the door creak open and closed she tried to open the locker. When she pushed on the door it didn't budge. She began running her fingers along the interior of the door for any kind of latch or release lever that would allow her to open it. The longer she searched the more panicked she became. She knew that the men wouldn't be outside long. If she stepped out of the locker just as they were coming back in she would be spotted.

Just when Ally's fingertips brushed across something that she thought might be the latch, she heard the door squeak open again. This time only one set of footsteps echoed through the factory. She heard the scraping sound again. She froze inside the locker and gave up on trying to find a way to get it open. Instead she focused on the sound of someone approaching the line of lockers. When he reached it he dropped something heavy and loud on the floor. Ally guessed it might have been a wooden crate. She could tell from the sound of his breath and subtle mutterings that he was right outside the locker. Only a thin sheet of metal separated them. Ally's stomach twisted as she anticipated what he would do when he opened the locker and found her.

Chapter Thirteen

Ally held her breath as she listened closely to the man on the other side of the locker door. Then the door jolted. Whoever was on the other side of it was tugging hard at the door. Ally closed her eyes, her teeth sunk into her bottom lip.

Her chest was tight with fear. The locker door shook again.

"What is wrong with this thing?"

Ally opened her eyes. She saw that the door was still closed. "Must be jammed," the man outside muttered. Ally drew a shallow, shaky breath. She hoped that the man would not hear it. She heard the clank of the next locker being opened. He shuffled something into the locker. Then he opened the next locker door. She heard more shuffling. Ally guessed that whatever the man had just purchased, was being stored in the lockers. She closed her eyes and hoped that he would not come back to the first locker and try to force it open. Ally's stomach churned as she heard his footsteps approaching her locker again. Luckily, he passed right by and continued walking.

Ally knew she wasn't safe yet, but she felt as if she was getting closer to the possibility. After a few more moments she heard the squeak of the door opening and closing again. She held her breath and stayed perfectly still. She listened harder than she had ever listened in her life. In the distance she could hear the faint rumble of a car engine. She nearly passed out from relief. She couldn't be sure, but she suspected that the man had left. How long would he be gone? Were others on their way? She had no idea. All she knew for sure was that she had to get out of the building as fast as she could. She jiggled the lever on the inside of the locker door. It did not budge. She pushed on it hard. The door still would not open.

"No!"

She shoved her entire body weight against it. It barely trembled. "No, no, no!" She pounded heavily on the inside of the door. Trapped inside of a tiny space, with no hope of getting out, she would be forced to wait for some criminal to find and execute her. Or worse yet, no one would ever find her. She hadn't told anyone where she was going. Why would they even look for her there?

With her heart pounding she knew that there was only one thing that she could do. She didn't want to put her grandmother in danger, but she was the only person that Ally could trust. Ally managed to maneuver her hand into her purse. She pulled out her phone and dialed her grandmother. When the phone rang, it sounded so loud through the ear piece. Her body tensed. What if the man hadn't left? What if he could hear what she was doing?

"Hello? Ally?"

"Mee-Maw, I need you to come to the old factory. But you have to be careful. It's dangerous. I'm trapped and I..."

A sharp beeping sound alerted Ally to the fact that the call had been dropped. She tried to dial again, but her grandmother must have still been on the line because the call went to voicemail. Ally tried again and saw that she no longer had service. Just then she heard the rustle of something not far from the lockers. It could have been an animal, or it could have been a person. Shocked by fear, Ally turned her phone off. She didn't want someone to hear it ring or vibrate if her grandmother called her. She had no idea if her grandmother had understood her. She didn't even know how much she might have heard before the call dropped. Was anyone going to come to help her? She stood perfectly still. She was too scared to wait, but too scared to start pounding again. She didn't want to draw attention to the fact that she was there, just in case someone dangerous was still close enough to hear. She had never been in any precarious situations in her life.

Her boring office job didn't involve hiding from dealers. Her dull husband's riskiest behavior was turning the channel when she was watching her favorite television show. The fear that coursed through her was far different than anything she had ever felt before. As she tried to get control of herself she knew that she might not be able to escape.

Ally leaned her forehead against the inside of the locker door and felt tears building in her eyes. She had made a huge mistake by running her own little investigation. She was either going to starve, or she was going to be killed. Those were not very good options for her to pick from. Being under so much pressure made her begin to get a little dizzy.

As the minutes slipped by she lost more and more hope. Then she heard the creak of the door. Ally was sure that it was over. The man had come back, or someone had arrived to pick up whatever he had stashed in the lockers. Either way if she was found she would be in a lot of danger. However, if she stayed trapped in the locker she might never have another chance to get out.

After several more seconds slipped by, Ally finally decided to take the risk.

Ally began pounding hard on the locker door.

"Ally?"

"Mee-Maw! Help me, I'm in here!" Ally nearly burst into tears with relief. She heard the subtle clack of her grandmother's low heeled shoes as she hurried over. Ally could hear her tugging at the door. "It's stuck," Ally wept.

"How did you even get in there?" Charlotte sighed. "Don't worry we'll get you out. You push and I'll pull and kick."

"You'll what?" Ally looked at the door.

"Do as I say, Ally!" Ally cringed at the tone in her grandmother's voice. It was one she had heard far too often as a child.

"Okay, ready!" Ally shoved her weight against the door. She could feel her grandmother tugging from the other side. Then she heard a loud clang. The door popped open and Ally fell out right into her grandmother's arms. "How did you do that?" Ally stared up at her with wonder.

"I've dealt with a stubborn locker or two. It usually takes a good, hard kick." Charlotte helped

Ally to stand up straight. "Now, do you want to tell me what you were doing in that locker?"

"I will, but not now. We have to get out of here before they come back." Ally jerked open the locker door beside the one she hid inside. When she saw what was hidden there she gasped with surprise.

"Cigarettes?" She stared at the packages with disbelief. "Why would they go to so much trouble to hide cigarettes?"

Charlotte peered inside the locker. "I bet that they're illegal cigarettes."

"Illegal cigarettes?"

"They get smuggled into the States because of the high tax on cigarettes. The worst part is they have no regulation. People buy these cigarettes without having any idea what is inside them."

"That's gross." Ally scrunched up her nose. "They could really just put anything in them?"

"Yes. Most people won't notice the difference. I saw a special about it. But I never would have guessed they'd be running them through a small town like Mainbry." She shook her head. "I guess people are right about the crime rate going up."

"There's no time to think about the crime rate of small towns, we have to get out of here before anyone comes back." Ally grabbed her grandmother's hand. As they rushed towards the door Ally's foot caught on something sharp. She lurched forward and caught herself on the handle of the door. When she looked down at what she had tripped on she saw that it was a small, silver case.

"What's this?" She leaned down to look at it.

"Ally don't!" Charlotte warned. "Just leave it alone and let's get out of here."

"But what if it's important to the case, Mee-Maw?" Ally frowned. Her mind filled with all of the possibilities of what might be inside. Not the least of which were the potential diamonds that she had imagined earlier. She tried to open the latches on the case, but they weren't budging.

"Ally, you're right, we need to go now."

Charlotte looked through the open door and down the driveway anxiously. "Anyone could show up at any moment."

Ally frowned and tried the latches one more time. Finally, they popped open. She lifted the lid of the case. What she saw inside had nothing to do with diamonds. It was a gun.

"Ally, put that down right this instant!" Charlotte demanded. Ally didn't think she could. She was mesmerized by the sight of it. Could it have been the weapon used to kill Connor? Had the man who left dropped it there? "Please, Ally put it back and let's go." Charlotte tugged at her arm. Ally snapped out of the state of shock. She knew that her grandmother had reason to be concerned. However, she couldn't imagine leaving the gun there for someone else to find or to use to hurt someone. She closed the latch on the box and used her other hand to guide her grandmother out of the building.

"I'll meet you at the cottage." Ally nodded towards the building. "My car is back there."

"Are you sure?" Charlotte frowned. "I'd feel better if you were with me."

"Me too, but if I leave my car here then whoever comes back will know who was snooping around." Ally gave her grandmother's hand a quick squeeze. "I'll be careful I promise."

"The gun?" Charlotte looked at the case.

"I'll take it to the police station. I'm not going to risk it disappearing or being used to hurt someone." Ally felt uneasy at the idea of actually taking it to the police station, but she thought it was her only option. She watched while her grandmother got into the van. Once she was safely driving away, Ally walked around the side of the building to the back. She hoped that neither of the men had noticed her car there. It didn't look like it had been disturbed. However, she did notice something odd as she moved closer to it. Tiny curls of wood shavings were piled up not far from where her car was parked. They stood out against the sun-ravaged pavement. There was no time to dwell on it. She hopped into the car and began driving.

Her first stop was going to be the police station to turn in the gun. However, as she drove the wood shavings stuck in her mind. She remembered that Luke had given her grandmother the tiny, wooden hummingbird for her collection. Was it possible that those had been the wood shavings left behind? If so then it was clear he had spent a lot of time at the old factory, which confirmed in her mind, yet again, that Luke had to be involved in what was happening at the factory. How would it look if she turned in a gun that she had found there? It would be like painting a target on her back. As uncomfortable as it made her to think of holding onto the gun, she didn't know what else to do with it. She decided she would consult with her grandmother for advice.

As Ally pulled into the driveway she saw her grandmother waiting outside for her. Despite the distance between them Ally could see the strain in her grandmother's expression. She knew that her grandmother was not at all pleased with what she had done. Although Ally had lived on her own for many years at times, she still felt like a scared child under her grandmother's scrutiny. With reluctant steps she made her way to the front of the cottage. She knew having the gun would only make things worse. Ally decided to keep the fact that she still had it to herself for the moment. Once she stepped inside the cottage, her grandmother began pacing back and forth with frustration.

"What were you thinking? Why would you go back to that place without telling anyone, without taking anyone with you? Do you know what kind of danger you were in? What if you hadn't had your phone? What if someone had found you before I did?" By the time she was done with the rant she was winded.

"Mee-Maw, I didn't think it would be dangerous. I just wanted to figure out what was happening there. No one else was looking into it. I wanted to be sure that my suspicions were right before I asked for help with it. Was I supposed to just let Brent get locked away for the rest of his life?" She crossed her arms. "How is that fair to him? He's innocent in all of this, I know he is!"

"What you're supposed to do is take your concerns to the police. That's what they're there for. That's what they're trained for. Brent could still be involved in all of this." Charlotte shook her head and stormed off towards the kitchen. "I don't think you should have gone there. You should have told Julian."

Ally followed after her grandmother. "How could I tell Julian? What happens if he doesn't believe me and he tips off Luke!"

Charlotte spun around to face her granddaughter. "You really think he would do that?"

"I don't know what to think anymore," Ally said feeling very perplexed. "It's all very confusing. How do you think he would react to me accusing his partner of a crime?" Ally cringed. "I don't think he'll believe me. He barely knows me, but he's with Luke day after day. They have to have some kind of relationship. Maybe Luke isn't involved after all, how would that make me look."

"You don't know until you try, Ally. It is possible that Julian won't believe you. But it's possible he will. If Luke is involved then Julian is in as much danger as we are. Even if he isn't involved we need to let them know about the men at the factory before someone else gets hurt. What if the men work out that you were at the factory? Then you will be in even more danger. If Luke and Julian don't know what's going on, who is going to protect you?"

"No one." Ally grimaced. "I can't even go to the patrol officers because the moment I mention Connor they're going to refer me to Luke and Julian. There's no way out of this, Mee-Maw, and I'm sorry that I pulled you into it."

"Ally honey, if you're in it I'm in it, too. There's no pulling needed. I want Connor to have justice, too. I just don't want to see you get hurt." She patted Ally's cheek. "Sweetheart, I hope that you know I am always here for you. I am always on your side. I just want to know that you're making the safest choice you can."

"I think there's only one way to know that." Ally sighed. "I'll look into it tomorrow. I need to think through a few things. I promise, I will be careful. Are you going to be okay at the shop by yourself?"

"Yes, but I hate to leave you alone. I can close up for the rest of the day."

"No, we need to keep everything as normal as possible. I don't want anyone involved to get suspicious, and your shop not being open will be suspicious."

"I guess you're right." Charlotte nodded. "But call me right away if you think of anything. I still think it would be best if you talked to Julian."

"I'll think about it." Ally turned and walked down the hall to her room. She tried to clear her mind with each step she took. She heard the front door close and knew that she was alone. She waited a few more minutes, then headed back out to her car. She grabbed the metal case that held the gun and carried it back inside the house. It was unnerving to have a weapon so close to her, especially the one that had likely killed Connor. She tucked it into her closet behind her suitcase where she hoped that it would be safe until she could figure out what to do. Then she sat down on her bed. Peaches nudged the bedroom door open. She jumped up into Ally's lap.

Ally stroked Peaches' fur and tried to settle her nerves. After being trapped inside a locker and nearly discovered by a criminal, possibly a murderer, it was hard to calm down. Peaches helped by purring and nuzzling Ally's hand. Now that she could relax and breathe she could try to make sense of what had happened. Her mind ran through what had happened at the factory. The first thing she remembered was the smell in the factory. She now knew the smell was the tobacco. Ally gasped as suddenly she knew that it was the same scent she had smelled on Julian.

"The question is, why would Julian smell like

the tobacco? Maybe he's been trying to figure out what Luke is up to? Maybe he followed Luke and picked up the smell on his clothes? Maybe he had been looking into the factory? If Luke is involved in something criminal like this Julian could be in serious danger." Ally stood up from the bed, causing Peaches to jump down. "I have to find out what is really happening with Julian. Does he suspect Luke? Does he know that Luke is innocent and I am completely off base? Does he have solid evidence against Brent that I don't know about? Could both Julian and Luke be involved in this? Could Julian be protecting Luke? Or is he just oblivious to Luke's involvement?" She needed to uncover the truth and she knew exactly what to do in order to do that.

"Peaches, I've got to talk to Julian. But I can't let him know that I know. If I do and he's more involved than I think, he might alert Luke, and then Mee-Maw and I could both be in danger."

Ally felt anxious about the idea of speaking to Julian. He was all charm on the surface, but she was worried that he was hiding something darker underneath. Why would he trust her over his partner? She stretched out on her bed. The morning had taken a lot out of her. Her body still ached from being stuck in one position for so long. She closed her eyes and continued to try to sort through her thoughts. She only succeeded in falling asleep.

Chapter Fourteen

When Ally woke a few hours later the sun was low. She knew it was getting close to evening. As she listened, she heard the sound of her grandmother moving things around in the garden. Whenever Charlotte was stressed she would garden. It had led to some very interesting plant designs. Ally sat up slowly. Her back still ached a little but she felt better than she had. Right away her mind began to spin. She decided it was time to confront Julian and find out what he knew about Luke. She would rather see him away from the police station, and more importantly away from Luke. As she stood up Peaches ran around her ankles. Ally knew that she was hungry. She walked out into the kitchen and set out some food and water for the cat. There were freshly baked rolls on the counter. Ally snatched one up.

She sighed and peeked out the window. She could see her grandmother was still working in the garden. Ally suspected that she was partly still out there to keep an eye on Ally. How was she going to slip past her?

"Honesty is always the best policy, right Peaches?" Ally reached down and scratched the cat's chin. "Or at least something close to it." Once Peaches had eaten she carried the cat and her water dish to her bedroom. Peaches was still kept inside because she wasn't used to her new surroundings, but she usually had free run of the cottage as Arnold spent most of his day outside. However, for the next few hours she was going to be stowed away in Ally's room. She made sure that Peaches had plenty of water then closed the door to her bedroom. With the plan forming in her mind she needed to be sure that the cat didn't escape. She grabbed her purse and headed out the door. As she expected, the moment she stepped outside her grandmother stood up.

"Where are you going, Ally?" Charlotte's tone had a friendly edge, but her eyes contained authority. Ally could tell that she was very worried about her. She paused in front of her grandmother and frowned. Charlotte straightened her shoulders as if she was preparing for a fight.

"I thought about what you said, Mee-Maw, and I decided that you're right." Ally managed a small smile.

"I am?" Charlotte smiled with relief.

"Yes. I've been going about this all wrong. I am going to visit Julian and tell him about everything. I should have done that in the first place." Ally gestured to her car. "I'm just going to drive over."

"Oh Ally, I think that is the best choice. If Luke is up to something Julian will handle whatever it is. You can just tell him everything and wash your hands of it. It will be for the best." Charlotte gave her a warm hug. "I'm glad you understood why I was so upset. I'm sure Julian will prove himself, and make sure that your name is kept out of all of this."

"I do, I really do understand, Mee-Maw. I know that you just want me to be safe. I'm going to try to make sure that this whole situation gets settled." She hugged her grandmother. "Make sure that you take Arnold for his walk, I saw him rooting around in the backyard."

"I will." Charlotte waved to Ally. "Let me know how it goes."

Ally climbed into her car and drove off down the street. As she drove she thought once more of the wood shavings. Had she just assumed that they were connected to Luke? They could have been from anything really. Maybe she was letting her paranoia get the better of her. Julian's house was on the other side of town. It wasn't exactly the rich side, but the houses were larger and the lawns were greener.

Ally parked her car a few blocks away from Julian's house. She wanted it to look like she was walking, but she also wanted her car close enough to get to it fast if she needed to escape. She walked along the sidewalk with a concerned frown.

"Peaches!" She clicked her tongue a few times. "Here kitty, here kitty!" As she neared Julian's house she raised her voice even louder. She noticed that his car was in the driveway. Was Luke there with him? She had no idea. As she had hoped, Julian's windows were open. It was a beautiful day, and the breeze carried easily to cool off the interior of the homes in the small town.

"Peaches! Peaches! Here kitty kitty!" Ally felt a little ridiculous calling for a cat that she knew was probably snoozing on her bed at the cottage, but she thought it was the best way to get Julian's attention. He already knew that her cat had a habit of escaping, so it would not be too hard of a story for him to believe. After the next shout, Julian's door swung open.

"Ally, is that you?" Julian said cheerfully.

She paused at the end of his driveway. "Oh Julian, I'm so glad to run into you! My cat, Peaches, got away from me. I thought I saw her run down this street, but now I can't find her!" She did her best to summon tears to her eyes. "I'm so worried, she's not used to this area yet. I'm scared she's going to get lost. What if she can't find her way home and I never see her again."

"Ally, it's okay, don't worry." He hugged her. Ally didn't smell anything on his shirt. Had she imagined the smell before? Had she imagined that connection between it and the smell of the tobacco in the old factory? "I'll help you look for her. Cats." He shook his head. "They're moody little creatures that's why I never got one myself."

"Thanks Julian. I'm sorry to pull you away from anything you might have been busy with." She looked apologetic.

"It's no trouble. I was taking a break from filling out paperwork. Getting Brent's case ready for trial."

Ally bit her tongue to keep from pointing out that she believed Brent had nothing to do with Connor's death.

"I've been chasing her all around town. I don't know if I can even call her anymore, my throat is so dry." She sniffled.

"Oh, do you want to come in and get a drink?

It might give Peaches a chance to come out of her hiding place. You could probably use a few minutes of rest." He smiled that charming smile that had made her heart dance in high school. She had to admit that it still did. She stared into his eyes for a moment. Please, she thought, don't be in the middle of all of this, Julian.

"Thanks, that would be great. I'm really parched."

"Come right in." Julian led her up the driveway to his house. Ally felt a little guilty for deceiving him. She wanted nothing more than to get inside his house and see if she could find anything that connected him to Luke and the criminal activity. She wanted to speak to him and try to find out if he knew anything about the illegal cigarettes, the factory and Luke's possible involvement? If she could prove that he was not involved in any way then she could trust him. Julian walked with her into the house. Ally noticed that the furniture was arranged in a symmetrical pattern. It appeared that everything had its perfect place, and everything was in it. She followed him into the dining room which faced an open kitchen.

"Here, just sit here for a moment." He gestured to a chair at the dining room table. Ally noticed how neat and tidy Julian's kitchen was. Her ex had been rather messy and expected her to keep everything clean. It was refreshing to her to see that Julian found cleanliness to be important. She sat down in the chair.

"Thanks Julian. I really appreciate you taking time out to help me. I'm sure that you have other things that you could be doing."

Julian popped open the fridge and grabbed two cans of soda. Ally wasn't much of a soda drinker, but she didn't protest. She was more interested in finding out what Julian knew than what she had to drink.

"Here you go." He set the can down in front of her. "Or would you like a glass with ice?"

"This is fine, thanks." Ally opened the soda and watched as Julian sat down across from her.

"It's really no bother, Ally. I needed a break from all of the paperwork. The whole town seems to have an opinion on the situation, and they love to call the police station about it. I just thought I'd do some work at home so that I could be away from all of that chaos." He shook his head. "I guess it's so much of a scandal that everyone wants to be involved."

Ally smiled a little. "Well, good thing we have such a good detective to rely on."

"I try." Julian grinned. He opened his can of soda. "So, how long are you staying in town?"

"I'm not sure really." Ally shrugged. "My job is pretty flexible and I have a lot of vacation time owing."

"Sounds like a great job to have." Julian groaned. "Detective work is not flexible."

"Actually, it's pretty tedious, I don't really enjoy it, but flexibility is one of its perks. At least your job isn't boring." She took a sip of her soda.

"It can be, trust me. But you're right, I do

enjoy it."

"Even when you're working with Luke?" Ally tried to be as casual as possible about how she asked the question.

"Oh, not a fan of Luke?" Julian smirked. "Well, I don't blame you. He is such a stickler, and he doesn't exactly have the friendliest demeanor. He's not a bad guy though."

Ally frowned.

"Really? He seems a little shady to me." Ally met Julian's eyes.

"I wouldn't say that. He's not looking to make friends, but he does his job. In fact sometimes it's hard to get him to just relax and not take everything so seriously." He took a long swallow of his soda. "You know sometimes you just have to let things go. You don't have to follow the letter of the law."

Ally shifted in her chair. She toyed with the top of her soda can. She heard what Julian said, but it made her uncomfortable. He acted as if

Luke was a stellar detective. Why would he act that way if he knew or suspected Luke was involved in smuggling? Maybe he had no idea?

"You don't think he might be hiding something?" Ally pressed. Julian's smile faded. He set down his can of soda.

"What are you getting at, Ally?"

"Nothing really. He just seems like he might be putting on a false front." She shrugged.

"Good at reading people are you?" Julian chuckled. "Maybe you should be my partner instead of Luke."

Ally smiled at his words. "I don't know if that's such a good idea."

A knock on the front door summoned Julian's attention. "I'll be right back." He stood up and went to answer the door. Ally really didn't want to finish the soda, but she didn't want to appear rude. She walked over to the sink and poured the contents down the drain. Then she looked around for a recycling bin. She saw a small trashcan, but she was a big believer in never throwing out a can. She opened the pantry beside the back door. Inside was a small, square box. It had other cans and plastic bottles in it. Pleased that she had found it, Ally dropped the can into the box. As she started to turn around something caught her eye. A box on the shelf. A box from 'Charlotte's Chocolate Heaven'. It looked exactly like the box of chocolates that was meant to be delivered on the day that Connor died. In shock, she reached out to pick it up.

"Ally."

She jumped at the sound of Julian's voice right behind her. The box fell from her hands and broke open. Tiny salted caramel chocolate roses scattered in all directions. There was no question that they were the same chocolates.

"Julian I..." Ally couldn't get any words out of her tightening throat.

"I really wish that you hadn't seen that." Julian sighed with dismay. "To be honest with you I should have just thrown them out, but your grandmother's chocolates are so good! I couldn't let them go to waste." He shook his head. "I guess this is all my fault. But what's done is done. Right Ally?"

Ally stared at him with building fear. The way he spoke was so calculated and even a little bit amused. It was unsettling to her.

"I know there's an explanation, Julian, you don't have to worry about me." Ally took a slight step back away from him.

"I really wish you hadn't seen that," Julian repeated as he stepped back from the pantry. "I mean, things could have been different." He swung the pantry door shut. Ally heard him put something against the door. At first she was too shocked to react. Then panic set in.

"Julian!" She tried to open the door, when it wouldn't budge she pounded on it. "What are you doing? Let me out!"

Julian didn't respond. A minute or so later Ally heard loud music begin to play in the house. She knew that it was to cover the sounds of her pounding and screaming.

"Julian, this is crazy! Let me out!" She slammed her body against the door. She kicked and punched it. The door did not budge. She had flashbacks of being stuck in the locker. At least the pantry was a larger space, but Julian knew she was there. What did he plan to do with her, or to her?

A sinking sensation rocked Ally's stomach as she realized that she had left her purse sitting on the table. Her cell phone was inside it. Unlike the day before when she had a lifeline to save her, now she had nothing. Not only that but no one would ever suspect Julian. In fact, she was still having a hard time believing that Julian had just locked her inside his pantry. Could she have been so wrong about him? Was he just as deeply involved in the crime taking place as Luke? Had he really been involved in Connor's murder? Tears sprung to her eyes at the thought.

Would Julian really have killed Connor just to protect an illegal cigarette smuggling ring? She blinked back her tears and tried to focus. The pantry was at least large enough for her to move around in. There were foodstuffs lined up on the shelves. She searched for anything that she thought might help her to get the lock open. In a panic she swept boxes and cans right off the shelves. There was nothing. She grabbed the knob and twisted it hard. It didn't even budge.

She knew that getting out of the pantry was going to be impossible. Even if she did, Julian was likely waiting right outside for her. Had he left? She could barely hear anything because of the music. Was he going to come back? What would he do with her? Ally's jaw clenched as it occurred to her that he might kill her. If he had killed Connor, why wouldn't he kill her, too? Her stomach ached with repulsion. The man she had a crush on from the time she was a young girl had turned out to be the complete opposite of what she expected. Would her childhood crush really kill her?

Chapter Fifteen

Ally stopped thinking about how to get out and started thinking about what she could use as a weapon. There was a giant can of creamed corn on a bottom shelf. She picked it up. It strained her muscles enough to make her believe that it could knock Julian out. Then it was only a waiting game. A terrifying, waiting game. Ally thought of all of the choices she had made that had landed her locked up in a pantry. What it all came down to was that her grandmother was right, yet again. A little more caution would have gone a long way to prevent her current situation.

The music continued to play. Ally's heart pounded. The door knob started to turn. Ally's stomach twisted with fear as she heard the key turn in the lock. The door swung open. Ally heaved the can of creamed corn at Julian's head. Julian ducked to the side and the can sailed right past him.

"Stupid move, Ally." He grabbed her hard by

the hair and pulled her out of the pantry. Ally ignored the pain in her scalp. It was her only chance to get away from him. She shoved her elbow into his side and stomped on his foot. In all of the movies she had seen this was all it took to escape the bad guy. However, Julian was a fit and muscular police detective that was used to restraining criminals. He easily twisted Ally in his grasp and pinned her back against his chest. He held her arms across her body and lifted her feet from the floor.

"Now you listen to me. We're going to go for a ride."

"No!" Ally screamed. "I'm not going anywhere with you, Julian!"

"Yes, you are. If you fight me, we're going to make a stop at your grandmother's place and invite her along. Is that what you want, Ally? You want your precious Mee-Maw to keep you company?" The snarl in his voice made Ally certain that he would follow through with the threat.

"No." Ally was so scared that the word sounded more like a squeak.

"So, you're going to behave?" Julian tightened his grasp on her.

Ally nodded. Her chest tightened to the point that it was painful to breathe. She didn't know if it was fear or his strong grip.

"Let's go." He pulled her towards the door. "When we get outside you need to walk slowly to the car. Act like you're happy to be with me." He met her eyes. "If you don't, then maybe you'll get someone's attention. Maybe they'll interfere. But who is going to believe you? Ally! She's going through a divorce, she's a little emotional, maybe she needs some medication to help her through these hallucinations. Can you believe what she accused Julian of doing?" He sneered at her. "No one will believe you over me, Ally. You'll get locked away in a mental institution, and I'll be free to take my anger out on Charlotte."

"No please!" Ally's heart raced.

"Behave," he ordered her. Then he released

his grasp on her. He held out his hand to her. It took Ally a moment to realize that he wanted her to hold it, as if they were friends, or more than that. It made her sick to even consider it. Not long before she had thought maybe they could be more than friends, but now all she could think of was escaping from him.

"Ally?" He glared at her. Ally curled her hand around his. Her hand was trembling. He tightened his grip on it to hide the shaking. Then he opened the door. When Ally saw the driveway she remembered her car was parked not far away. She considered whether she would be able to make it to the car before Julian could catch her. He gave her hand a firm tug and she was reminded of the consequences of her actions. Julian wasn't going to let her escape. He hadn't let Connor escape.

When they reached the car Julian opened the passenger side door. Ally heard a car door slam closed at the same time. Her eyes lifted in the direction of the sound. Anxiety flooded her as she saw Luke walk up the driveway. In his jeans and taut t-shirt he looked harmless and handsome. But Ally knew that behind those reflective sunglasses was a ring leader. Was he there to finish the job for Julian?

"Behave," Julian hissed beside her ear. "Hi Luke." He smiled.

Anxiety gave way to confusion that made Ally just as dizzy. Luke nodded at Julian and then looked towards Ally.

"Ally."

When he said her name Ally's entire body sparked. She didn't know why. Was it fear? Was it hope?

"I don't know anything, Luke, I swear!" Ally's words spilled from her lips before she could even think them through. Julian squeezed her hand so hard that Ally thought her fingers might break. Luke reached up and took off his sunglasses. His expression was as devoid of emotion as always.

"What?" He stared at her.

"She's a little drunk." Julian chuckled. "That's why I'm giving her a ride home."

"I thought you were working on paperwork?" Luke didn't look away from Ally, though he spoke to Julian. Ally's fogged mind began to put together that Luke didn't seem to know what Julian was up to. Did that mean that Julian hadn't told him that she had found the chocolates? Did that mean that he didn't know that she knew about the illegal cigarettes?

"Oh I was, but then Ally stopped by, and we had a few drinks. This girl can't hold her liquor. Never could." He winked at Ally. "Isn't that right, sweetheart?"

Ally swallowed thickly, her mouth was so dry. She had no idea what to do. She could only hope that Julian was hiding the truth from Luke because he was planning to let her go, instead of allowing Luke to kill her.

"Yes," she struggled to get the word out.

Luke continued to stare at her, hard. "Well, I can take her home. Then you can finish the paperwork. It has to be in by tomorrow."

"No!" Julian tugged Ally closer to him. "I mean, she doesn't know you very well."

"And?" Luke laughed. "You think I'm going to hurt you, Ally?" He looked at Ally with amusement in his eyes.

When he laughed his expression became warm. Ally had never seen him look so friendly before. He didn't seem dangerous or cold at all when he looked at her. In the back of her mind she wondered if the assumptions she had made about Luke were wrong.

"Ally?" Luke took a step closer to her. "You all right?"

"Why wouldn't she be all right?" Julian frowned. "Get in the car, Ally." He released her hand so that she could get in the car. For a split-second Ally thought about flinging herself into Luke's arms. She could imagine feeling an immense sense of relief when he wrapped his arms around her. But she knew that Julian was right. No one would believe her, least of all Luke, who even suspected her of being involved in Connor's death. She couldn't risk what Julian might do to her, or her grandmother. She also didn't know if she could trust Luke.

"I'm fine," Ally managed to say. "But if you could check on my grandmother. Let her know that my cat, Peaches, is missing. I can't find her anywhere. She should get her favorite toy from my bedroom and use it to find her. Maybe you could help her look, Luke. Would you do that?" Ally looked at him with as much fear as she could contain in her eyes. She could only hope that he would get the message. She had locked away Peaches to make sure that she didn't actually escape, but now she needed someone to realize that she was in trouble. This was the only way that she could think of doing that. If Luke went to the cottage looking for her missing cat and her grandmother found her hidden in her room, then there would be no question that Ally had lied about the cat being missing. Hopefully that would be enough to get her grandmother's attention. But that would only work if Luke actually went to tell her grandmother to look for the cat.

"Well, I don't usually make house calls for cats." Luke rubbed the back of his neck.

"Ally, don't be silly, I'm taking you home right now," Julian reminded her. There was a subtle growl of warning in his tone. Ally gulped as she had forgotten about Julian's lie. "Once you're settled into bed, I'll help Charlotte find your cat. I promise you that. Now get in the car."

Instantly she heard the threat in Julian's voice. He wasn't just going to take care of her, he was going after her grandmother and even Peaches, too. She knew that she had to find a way to protect them.

"No Julian, please. I can't let her see me like this. She'll be so upset. Luke will go and check on her, right? Won't you, Luke?" Ally looked at the man who she had been suspicious of since the day she met him. She pleaded with him silently for help, with little hope that he would actually follow through. She needed him to. If Luke was at the house then Julian wouldn't be able to hurt her grandmother. At least that was what Ally hoped.

"Fine, I guess. But aren't you a little old to be worried about getting in trouble with your grandmother?" Luke offered her a wry smile. Ally didn't bother to respond. She doubted he would believe her story or even go speak to her grandmother.

"In the car, Ally," Julian instructed her through gritted teeth.

Ally eased herself into the passenger seat. As Julian shut the door she had a terrible feeling that she wasn't going to get out of the car alive. She looked out the window to where Luke stood, but he had already walked away. Her last hope faded. She closed her eyes as Julian climbed into the car beside her.

"I know what you tried to do there. Not wise, Ally." He started the car. Ally reached for the door handle, but it was locked. She went to unlock it, but the lock was broken off. Julian smirked at her and began to back down the driveway. Ally could see Luke sitting in his car parked beside the driveway watching them leave. Julian drove right out of town. It didn't take Ally long to recognize the path. He was taking her to the factory. She tried to remain calm. There was no point in fighting.

Chapter Sixteen

Charlotte walked up to the cottage with Arnold snorting and rooting the entire way. She knew that he had something he was trying to search out, but she was impatient. She still hadn't heard from Ally and was starting to worry. When she looked up at the front door of the cottage she saw Luke Elm waiting for her. The sight of him made her breath catch in her throat. He was handsome, young enough to be her grandson, but that wasn't what had startled her. It was the knowledge that he was likely a killer. Luke turned to face her. His face was tight with concern.

"Hello Charlotte."

"Hi." Charlotte walked closer to him. Arnold continued to root. "What are you doing here, Luke?"

"Ally asked me to let you know that her cat is missing." He focused on the pig that was snorting at his shoes.

"Peaches is missing?" Charlotte looked puzzled. "I didn't know that." She opened the door to the cottage. "Why didn't she call me?"

"Uh." Luke wagged his head back and forth. "She was a little occupied."

Charlotte narrowed her eyes. She knew that he was hiding something. "Really?"

"Anyway, if you need help looking for the cat, I could look with you." Luke seemed awkward about the offer. Charlotte got the feeling that he was well aware that she was not very fond of him.

Just then they both heard a loud meow from inside the cottage. "Peaches?" Charlotte stepped inside. Arnold trotted in as well. He never turned down the opportunity to curl up on the rug. However, he made a bee-line straight for Ally's room. The meowing continued.

"It sounds like she's in Ally's room." Charlotte laughed. "I guess she's not missing after all."

She opened the door to Ally's bedroom. Peaches stood by the door ready to race out.

Arnold snorted right in her face. Peaches snarled and ran straight for the closet. Arnold ran straight after her.

"Oh dear!" Charlotte held onto the leash, but it was long enough for Arnold to reach the closet. Luke stood staring at the entire fiasco with a shocked expression.

"Well, don't just stand there, help me get the pig!" Charlotte demanded.

Luke blinked at her. "You want me to touch it?"

"It's just a pig, city boy, it's not going to hurt you." Charlotte had to laugh at the horror in his eyes. Luke cleared his throat. He moved a little closer to the pig. Arnold was no longer paying any attention to Peaches. He had found something more interesting in the back of the closet. He was rooting and snorting as he bumped his nose against something hidden.

Luke reached down in an attempt to wrangle the pig. The pig snorted, squirmed, and backed up.

"What's this?" Luke asked. He stood up holding the silver case that Ally had found at the old factory. Just as Charlotte opened her mouth to make up a lie and tell him not to touch Ally's personal things, the case popped open and the gun inside tumbled out. It landed on the floor.

"Watch out!" Luke shouted. He jumped in front of Charlotte. "It could have gone off," he growled. "Do you know how irresponsible it is to keep a gun like this?" He snatched the gun up off the floor. Charlotte stared at him with confusion.

"You don't know whose it is?"

"I'm assuming it's Ally's if it's in her closet, and I will be speaking to her about proper storage and gun safety." Luke shook his head. "Are you aware of how many accidental deaths there are..."

"Wait." Charlotte's eyes widened. "Why would Ally say that Peaches was missing if she knew that she had closed her up in her room?"

"I'm not sure." Luke frowned. "She was a little uh, intoxicated."

"Intoxicated?" Charlotte shook her head. "That's impossible. Ally doesn't get drunk, even if she did, she couldn't have. She's only been out of the house for about an hour."

"Well, she didn't want you to know." A faint blush arose in Luke's cheeks. "She seemed embarrassed."

"Who was she with?" Charlotte's tone shifted from confused to concerned.

"Don't worry, she was with Julian. She asked him not to bring her home. So maybe they went to a friend's." He shrugged. "At least the cat is safe. But this gun..."

"No, no, no!" Charlotte gasped. "This is all wrong. Ally never would have said that Peaches was missing if she wasn't."

"She begged me to come here and tell you." Luke frowned.

"She must have been trying to tell me something!" Charlotte wrung her hands. "Oh no, she must be in trouble."

"I think you're getting a little ahead of yourself, Charlotte. She was with Julian, I'm sure she's fine." He narrowed his eyes. "They were probably reuniting."

"No," Charlotte spoke firmly. "Luke, are you sure you don't know anything about that gun?"

"What am I supposed to know?" Luke asked.

"Ally found it at the old factory." Charlotte braced herself for his reaction. If Luke was the criminal they had both suspected, then she had just given away that they were on to him.

"The old factory?" Luke took a step closer to her. "What was she doing out there? Why didn't she turn the gun in?"

Charlotte swallowed thickly. She still couldn't be sure that Luke was trustworthy. "She wasn't sure who to trust with it."

Luke searched Charlotte's eyes. "Are you implying that she doesn't trust me?"

"I'm not implying anything." Charlotte shook her head. "But I know if Ally went to so much trouble to get you here to tell me to look for Peaches, who wasn't missing at all, then something is very wrong. We need to find her before she's hurt, or worse."

"Why would Julian hurt her?" Luke's eyes widened. "You know, don't you?" Charlotte felt the heat drain from her face. She looked at him wordlessly. Luke stepped closer to her. Charlotte backed into the wall in an attempt to escape him. "What do you know, Charlotte?"

Luke still held the gun in one hand. The gun she believed had killed Connor. Charlotte's heart pounded as she stared into his eyes.

"You should go," Charlotte stammered out. She edged towards the door. Luke shook his head. He pushed the door to Ally's bedroom closed.

"We're not going anywhere until you tell me why Ally hid this gun, and everything that the two of you think you know."

Chapter Seventeen

The car jolted to a stop. Ally was quite aware that the factory was isolated and empty. She knew that even if she screamed, no one would hear her or come for her. There were no neighbors for miles, and even if there were, they would likely mind their own business. Her only option was to flee. But she didn't think that she could outrun Julian. He was in incredible shape and he had played every sport in high school. Ally was slender, but not exactly fit. She preferred reading to running and had no idea how long her stamina would last. Julian turned the car off and looked over at her with a mild smile. The way he seemed to be enjoying their encounter made her even more concerned.

"So, do you know where we are?"

Ally remained quiet. Now that she was sure that Julian had murdered Connor, she assumed that he was involved in the illegal cigarette smuggling. Julian didn't wait for an answer. He got out of the car and walked around to the passenger side. Ally waited until he had unlocked the door from the outside. Then she slammed all of her weight against the door. The door swung hard into Julian's stomach and chest. He gasped at the unexpected strike, but he did not fall back as Ally had hoped. When she saw that he didn't budge, Ally lunged for the driver's side door. She just managed to get the door open, when Julian stepped up in front of her. He grabbed her by the shoulders and pulled her out of the car and onto the floor.

"Stop being so difficult!" His voice roared above her head. The fact that he wasn't worried about being heard just reminded her that there was no hope of being rescued.

"Please Julian. I'm not going to tell anyone. Just let me go." Ally looked up at him with wide eyes. "We practically grew up together! How can you do this to me?"

"We grew up together?" Julian laughed. "No, Ally. You were nothing when you were a kid, and you're nothing now. Just the scrawny, quiet girl that mooned over me every time she saw me."

Ally stared at him with disbelief.

"Oh, did you think I didn't know about your ridiculous crush? You still have it don't you, Ally?" He laughed and shook his head. "Pathetic. Did you really think something was going to happen between us?" He laughed cruelly. "You really are as crazy as your grandmother. But it doesn't matter now. You're going to pay for being as nosy as you are. All you had to do was let it go. If you had minded your own business, none of this would have happened."

Ally swallowed back a scream. There was no question that Julian had no interest in letting her go. Julian pulled her into the factory and closed the door behind him. Ally strained against his grasp and twisted, but Julian barely noticed. Julian carefully looked over the interior of the factory. She guessed that he was making sure that no one else was there. Then he led her over to the lockers. For a moment Ally was worried that he would force her inside the locker again. Then she remembered that he had no idea that she had ever even been there. He hadn't been one of the two men in the factory earlier that day.

"So, all of this for some illegal cigarettes?" Ally spat out her words with disgust. "You're going to murder two people over some tobacco? How much can you possibly get out of that?"

Her words grabbed Julian's attention. He looked sharply back at her. "What do you know about that?"

"I know that those lockers are full of illegal cigarettes. I know that you've been allowing the smuggling of cigarettes. How much do you get for selling out your neighbors, Julian?" Ally could see the fury that she was stirring up inside of him. She didn't care. If she wasn't going to make it out of the factory alive, she wanted to make sure that Julian knew what she thought of him. "That's pretty low, Julian. You have the nerve to pretend that you're protecting your community when all you're actually doing is corrupting it."

"Shut your mouth!" Julian snarled. "It's what had to be done."

"Oh? Murdering Connor, someone you went to school with, your neighbor's son, had to be done?" She scowled at him. "Did you do it, or were you too much of a coward? Did Luke have to do it for you?"

Julian stared at her with an emptiness in his eyes. "It doesn't matter now, does it?"

"Then to make it worse you tried to frame Brent for it?" Ally shook her head.

"It was Brent or your grandmother." Julian smirked. "But Brent was easier." Ally's heart raced as she recalled that Peaches had escaped from the cottage through a back door that had been left open. Had Julian sneaked into the cottage in an attempt to plant evidence? She shivered at the thought.

"Brent had nothing to do with any of it, did he?"

"Of course not." Julian smirked. "Brent

wouldn't be clever enough to be involved in something that would set him up financially for the rest of his life."

"Julian, you're disgusting."

"You're going to judge me?" Julian laughed. "What a joke! Blue River isn't anything to protect. It's a bunch of going nowhere people in a dying town. I wasn't about to let myself get stuck here. All I have to do is keep the route open for a few years and I'll have enough money to move away from this place and live a life of luxury. Just like you did, Ally. Just like most of the kids we grew up with did. Nobody wants to get stuck here."

"But don't you even think about the people you grew up with? The neighbors that looked after you? You're bringing danger into their backyards!" Ally shook her head. "No one deserves that."

"I don't care what anyone deserves. Neighbors who looked after me? The only person who cares about me, is me, Ally. I learned that a long time ago, and I'm not about to let anyone stop me from getting what I want. Nothing will prevent me from getting the life I want. Connor tried, and now you are, too. I don't feel bad about it, not one bit. So, you can give up on trying to convince me. All it does is give me a good chuckle." He grinned.

Ally stared at him with disbelief. Never would she have imagined that Julian could be so cruel.

"You had me fooled." She closed her eyes. A deep sense of regret welled up within her. "Just get it over with."

She felt Julian's fingertips brush across her forehead. "It's a shame really. If you hadn't found what you did, we could have played a game for a while. We could have had something. Instead, you had to go where you weren't invited."

"Just leave my grandmother out of this please. She doesn't know anything about any of this." Ally opened her eyes and looked directly into his. "At least promise me that you won't harm her."

"Aw, that's so kind of you, Ally. Such a good

granddaughter you are." He smiled with a sweet flutter of his eyes. "Too bad I don't care about you or your grandmother! I don't owe you anything. If your grandmother gets in my way, she will get the same thing Connor did. But first, it's your turn." He reached out and wrapped his hands around her throat. Ally grabbed at his wrists. She scratched as hard as she could. Julian didn't even seem to notice. He only tightened his grip on her throat. In her desperation she thought she saw the door swing open. Light filled the entrance of the factory. She mistook it for the spiritual light that so many people claimed to have seen at the point of death. As beautiful as it was, she still had the urge to fight, if only to protect her grandmother.

"Julian, what are you doing?" The voice boomed throughout the factory. It came from all directions as if it surrounded Ally. Julian's grasp on her throat relaxed just enough for her to steal a breath. Her sight cleared with the return of oxygen. She watched as Luke stepped further into the factory. He glared in their direction.

"Help!" Ally squeaked out, despite how raw her throat was from struggling to breathe. She didn't hold out much hope that Luke would help her. In fact he didn't even look directly at her. He kept his eyes on Julian. Was he angry about Julian hurting her, or was he angry that he hadn't already taken care of the job?

"Luke, this is not your concern! Just a little lover's spat!" Julian insisted. His hands fell back to his sides. "You know how girls get when they're drunk." He shrugged.

"She's coming with me." Luke gestured to Ally to walk towards him. Ally didn't dare to move a muscle. She was starting to believe that Luke might be there to help her, but she didn't want to risk angering Julian.

"You don't want to go with him, do you, Ally?" Julian's voice dripped with sweetness. "You want to stay here with me, and finish what we started. You wouldn't want your grandmother to find out the truth, to know what really happens to those who get into other people's business."

Ally felt tears biting at the back of her eyes. She knew that Julian was threatening her grandmother again. Luke moved a little closer to the two. He held his hand out to Ally.

"Come to me, Ally, I'll take you home."

Ally searched his face for any hint of what his intentions were. She had thought she could trust Julian, but she had been wrong. Now she had no idea what to think of Luke. Before she could make a choice, Julian wrapped his arm around Ally's throat. He began to squeeze hard. Ally felt her breath leave her again.

"Luke, you should have stayed out of this." Julian jerked Ally's body closer to his and increased the pressure on her throat. "If you take a step closer she's dead."

Luke immediately backed off a few steps. He reached towards his pocket.

"No phones!" Julian barked. "Do you think I'm that stupid?"

"Julian, what are you doing here?" Luke

stared hard at him. "You're throwing away your career, your freedom, for what?"

"I'm not throwing away anything." Julian increased the pressure on Ally's throat. "I'm doing what has to be done."

"Julian, you're going to kill her! Let her go!" Luke spoke sharply.

"Julian, you're going to kill her," Julian's voice was mocking. "I'll never understand how guys like you get to be detectives. In my book you've got to have the ability to do whatever it takes to earn a badge."

"Julian, stop!" Luke demanded as he stepped forward.

"Don't do it!" Julian warned.

"Get your hands off her!" Luke growled with fury. He lunged at Julian. Julian snarled and thrust Ally to the ground. Ally watched as the two men began wrestling on the floor as she struggled to get to her feet. She could see the open door of the factory. Her only goal was to get out the door before Julian overcame Luke. Somewhere in the back of her mind she was aware that Luke had come to her rescue.

"Don't make me do it, Julian." She heard Luke shout with venom. Something about it made her freeze in the doorway. She turned to see that Luke had his gun pressed against Julian's chest. Julian looked up at Luke and laughed. He laughed so long and hard that Ally felt dizzy from the sound. It was not a normal laugh, nothing she had ever heard before. Luke easily flipped Julian over and pinned him down with his knee in the small of the man's back.

Ally watched as he began putting handcuffs on Julian. The metallic snap of the cuffs drew her out of her dazed state. She turned and ran again. All she could think of was getting back to her grandmother to make sure that she was safe. It didn't occur to her that she had no car, and that the distance was too far for her to run. She was in no state to run. Every breath she took made her throat feel as if it was on fire. Still, the compulsion to run pounded through her mind.

"Ally stop!" Luke's voice chased after her. Ally stumbled down the driveway towards the road. "Ally, I'm trying to help you!"

Keep going Ally, it was all she could think. But as she set one foot out onto the road her entire body grew weak. Her legs could no longer hold her. She began to fall. Ally's eyes fluttered as she felt strong arms seize her around the waist. Luke drew her close against his chest before she could hit the ground. Ally gazed up into his beautiful eyes, framed by the creases of worry lines. The last thing she saw was just how handsome he was.

Chapter Eighteen

In the distance Ally could hear sirens. They seemed very far away. She tried to open her eyes, but she couldn't.

"Help," she mumbled.

"It's all right now. Rest now." She felt hands on her body, maneuvering her chin and shoulders. Somehow there was bumping as if the whole world was shaking. Finally she was able to open her eyes. Only then did she realize that she was in an ambulance. The sirens that still sounded so distant were actually all around her. She stared at the person beside her for a moment. When she saw that it was a paramedic and not Luke she closed her eyes. Was she safe? It seemed much too daring to think that she was. She was alive and that was enough for now.

Ally felt the subtle rock of the ambulance rolling over the road. Her mind began to ease, or maybe it was the painkillers. Either way she felt calmer than she had in a long time. She attempted to sort through everything that had happened. It was all too confusing. Her mind kept shifting back to the one pressing question that she had. Was her grandmother safe? At some point during the trip she slipped back into unconsciousness.

In the hospital Ally began to surface more. She blinked her eyes in an attempt to gain focus. Everything appeared blurry and not quite as she remembered. She became aware of where she was because of the scent and the bright lighting. She had made it to the hospital. She was still alive. She was starting to think that she just might be safe. She sensed that someone was close to her, but she couldn't quite get her head to turn to look.

"Ally!" The familiar warmth of her grandmother's lips against her forehead didn't feel different at all. It felt the same as it had her entire life. She sighed with relief at the comfort of her grandmother's presence.

"Mee-Maw, I'm okay." Ally tried to push herself up. Pain shot through her body in response to the attempt.

"No you don't," the nurse that walked into the room spoke in a commanding voice. "You need to stay still until you're completely checked out."

Ally could finally relax as her grandmother's hand slid into hers. "Julian?" She turned her head towards her grandmother.

"Luke is taking care of him." Charlotte smiled at her granddaughter.

"I'm sorry, Mee-Maw."

"Oh, my sweet girl, there is absolutely nothing for you to apologize for. You were brave and you fought for justice. I'm proud of you, Ally, and so very grateful that you are okay. Sending Luke to tell me about Peaches was pure genius."

Charlotte gazed at her as if she had never seen anything more valuable. Ally was warmed to the core by her grandmother's love. She suddenly knew that was what had been missing from her life. She wanted to be near her family again, near the one person in the world who knew her inside and out.

"What about Luke?" Ally frowned. "I know he saved me, I know he did."

"Well, you know how much I hate to admit it when I'm wrong, but this time I have to. I was wrong. Luke was never involved in any of the smuggling. He became suspicious of Julian because when rumors came up about illegal cigarettes being funneled through Blue River, Julian would insist on investigating them by himself, but he said he never found anything. Luke started following Julian to see what he was up to. That was when he started looking into the old factory."

"Luke knew?" Ally asked with surprise.

"Yes. He told me that he staked out the old factory a few times. He suspected that Julian was involved, he just didn't know how involved. He was working on getting the evidence, but then Connor was murdered and he strongly believed that Julian might be in some way responsible, but he needed the proof before he could take any further action against him. It is such a serious thing to accuse another police officer. He also didn't want to tip Julian off that he suspected him, but he never thought it would put you in danger."

"I feel terrible." Ally frowned. "The whole time I thought it was Luke that was dodgy."

"I suspected him too, Ally. Don't feel bad. Being in a small town can make you suspicious of outsiders. The important thing is that it's all being sorted out now. Connor's mother will have the closure that she needs, and our town will be safer." She stroked the back of Ally's hand. "And you are safe. I intend to keep you that way."

Ally smiled at her grandmother.

"Now, get some rest. If you behave the doctors might let you come home tonight."

Ally nodded and closed her eyes. She really did think of going to the cottage as going home. There was nowhere else in the world to which she had such strong feelings of attachment. After a few more hours of being under observation, Ally was awake again. She was relieved to see her grandmother was still by her side.

"You're looking good." The nurse smiled as she walked over to Ally. "I think you'll do fine at home, as long as you promise to rest."

"I promise."

"Before I release you there's someone that would like to speak with you." The nurse gestured to the door. Ally looked towards the door, hoping that it would be Luke. She wanted to thank him for what he had done and apologize for the way she had acted towards him. Instead it was Amelia Nissle.

"Hi Ally." She stepped into the room.

"Amelia, hi." Ally managed a smile.

"I know that you're resting, but I wanted to let you know how grateful I am. I heard about what happened, and I just couldn't wait to speak to you. You really believed in my brother, when no one else in the town did." She pulled a tissue out of her pocket and wiped at her eyes. "I thought he was going to jail for the rest of his life. Instead he'll be home soon, thanks to you."

"It wasn't just me." Ally shook her head.

"It was you." Amelia smiled warmly at her. "You chose to have faith in Brent even though almost everyone else suspected him. You did something to help him. I know my brother isn't the boy he used to be, he's done some not so great things in life, but you still saw him for who he is. I see him that way, too. That means a lot to me, Ally, and to our family. If there's anything that we can do for you, all you have to do is ask."

"There might be one thing." Ally sat up slowly. Charlotte looked over at her curiously.

"What is it?" Amelia stepped closer to the bed.

"Get your family and Connor's family to end all of this fighting. That way Connor's death will mean something." Ally nodded. "I think Connor would have liked that."

"I do, too." Charlotte patted Ally's hand.

"I'll do what I can," Amelia promised them both. "Thanks again, Ally."

After Amelia left the hospital room Ally began to get ready to leave. She couldn't help but wonder why Luke hadn't come by to speak to her. She knew that he was probably busy with the case. She hoped that it wasn't because he was upset with her. Not that he didn't have plenty of reason to be upset. After all she had suspected him of being a murderer and a smuggler as well as a crooked detective. The more she thought about it, the more she realized that he probably wanted nothing to do with her, which was a very big problem for Ally, because she couldn't stop thinking about him.

"Are you okay, Ally?" Charlotte asked.

"I think so." Ally frowned.

"Really?" Charlotte raised an eyebrow.

"All right, I'm a little worried about Luke." Ally sighed. "I really hope he's not upset with me."

"Ally, he saved your life, remember?" Charlotte smiled. She wheeled the wheelchair down the hall.

"I know he did. But that's what detectives do."

Ally stared wistfully into the night as she left the hospital. She had been so preoccupied with Julian's charm and her childhood crush that she had overlooked the presence of a true hero. She hoped that she would not make that mistake again.

Chapter Nineteen

Ally woke up the next morning with a fright. For just a moment she thought she was still trapped in Julian's pantry. As that sense of fear faded she recalled the way she had been rescued the day before. Just the thought of Luke made her buzz with excitement. She had been completely wrong about him. She was just grateful that he had come to her rescue when she needed him the most.

The scent of coffee wafted beneath her nose. Ally could hear the subtle noises of her grandmother in the kitchen. Peaches lifted her head from where she was tucked in the crook of Ally's arm. She nuzzled the curve of Ally's neck.

"Peaches, what a wild experience. Thanks to you, I got out of it. What would I do without you, kitty cat?" She smiled at the cat. Peaches wiggled her whiskers as if she was a bit exhausted by Ally's antics. Ally giggled at the thought. She took a few more minutes to pet Peaches. She was very grateful for the solace the cat offered her. When she couldn't ignore the delicious smell anymore she decided it was time to get up. Slowly she rose out of bed.

With her body still stiff and sore from the struggle the day before she found it much easier to just grab a robe than to change out of her pajamas. She pulled it on and didn't bother to look in the mirror or brush her hair. She was looking forward to just relaxing over breakfast with her grandmother. When she opened the bedroom door Peaches bolted out and headed straight for the kitchen. She knew that it was time for breakfast. Ally followed after her with a smile on her face.

When Ally stepped into the kitchen, she froze. Not only was her grandmother pouring three cups of coffee, but Luke was sitting at the kitchen table. He turned when he heard her in the doorway. He smiled at her when she stepped into the kitchen. Ally could not bring herself to smile back. She was mortified. She hadn't brushed her hair, or washed her face and the robe she was wearing was from her college days. She couldn't imagine how she must look to him. Poor Luke had no idea what he would face when he showed up far too early for a visit.

"Ally, I'm glad you're awake." Charlotte smiled at her. She could tell that Ally was uncomfortable. "Coffee?" She held the mug out to her.

"I didn't know we had company, I'm sorry. Let me go get changed." Ally started to retreat from the kitchen.

"Don't even think about it," Luke warned. He stood up from the table and pulled a chair out for her. "I don't want you moving more than you have to. You need to rest. If you want me to leave I will, but I wanted to update you on the situation." He gestured to the table. "Will you sit with me for a minute?"

Ally felt uncomfortable at the idea of sitting beside him in her frumpy pajamas, but she didn't want to miss out on the update. She also didn't want to insult him more than she already had. She sat down in the chair across from him. "Okay, what's going on?"

"Well, Julian has been arrested. He gave up the entire smuggling ring, so trust me, he's safer in jail." Luke shook his head. "He was mixed up with some really dangerous guys. He had no idea how far in over his head he had gotten himself."

"I don't think he minded." Ally's eyes narrowed. "I've never known anyone so cruel."

"You didn't feel that way before." Luke took a sip of his coffee, but his eyes remained on her.

"I guess I didn't know him at all." She sighed and looked into Luke's eyes. "The same way I didn't know you. Luke, I'm very sorry about the way I acted towards you."

"No need to be." He smiled at her. "It's not as if I was the pillar of friendliness. To be honest I had no idea who might be involved. If Julian was in the middle of everything, I figured there might be a lot of other people in town that were involved, too. That's why I was distant with everyone. I wanted to have an unbiased opinion and not scare Julian off so he covered his tracks."

"That makes sense." Ally nodded. "I just wish I had taken the time to get to know you instead of jumping to conclusions."

"I wish I had given you more reason to trust me. Great thinking about the story about the cat."

Ally laughed a little. "Yes, I didn't know what else to do. I just wanted to be sure that my grandmother was safe."

"Such a good girl," Charlotte cooed at her and pecked her on the cheek. "I'm going to check on Arnold."

As she stepped out the back door Ally knew that she was just making an excuse to leave the two of them alone.

"I'm glad Julian is finally behind bars where he can't hurt anyone else."

"Me too." He stared down at the mug of coffee that Charlotte had set in front of him. "You know, that's not even why I'm here, Ally."

"It's not?" Ally looked at him. "Then why?"

He looked up at her and released a heavy sigh. "I came to apologize."

"Apologize?" Ally laughed a little. "Why would you apologize to me? You saved my life."

"Maybe." He sat back in his chair. "But I can't believe that I let Julian get away with what he was doing for so long. I should have taken more action sooner, but Mainbry isn't my jurisdiction and if I went to the Mainbry police with what I suspected I needed proof. I needed to have enough evidence to bring him down if he was guilty and not antagonize him if he wasn't. I didn't want to blow the case and allow the possibility that he might get away with murder. I guess I also didn't want to believe that he could have been involved in this."

In that moment Ally became aware of just how seriously Luke took his job. What she had mistaken for a cold attitude, had more to do with determination and focus. Ally reached across the table and rested her hand on top of Luke's. Despite her familiar movement, he didn't pull his hand away. "Luke, I've known Julian all of my life, and up until the moment you saved my life, I believed that you were the one behind all of this."

"Me?" Luke's expression crumpled with offense. "Why would you think that?"

"I might have helped a bit with that," Charlotte admitted as she stepped back into the kitchen. "You know small towns aren't too kind to outsiders, Luke. I think it's Ally and I that owe you an apology."

"You're right." Ally nodded. "I had no real reason to suspect you, Luke, and I should have taken the time to get to know you instead of letting my imagination run wild."

"Ally, I understand. I wasn't exactly friendly." Luke smiled. "I guess we both had the wrong idea about each other. I thought you were trying to pit Connor and Brent against each other as some kind of rebound to get over your divorce."

"You know about that?" Ally asked. She laughed at the idea of her pitting the two men against each other.

"Julian might have mentioned it a few times." He shrugged.

"The entire town is talking about it." Charlotte rolled her eyes. "There's nothing more juicy than a good old scandal."

Ally shook her head. "There are no secrets in a small town. Well, I guess that's not exactly true. Julian certainly kept his criminal behavior a secret."

"Now Julian will pay for what he did. Brent is in the process of being released and all charges against him will be dropped." Luke took a sip of his coffee.

"There's going to be a lot of people in this town that owe him an apology, too." Charlotte stirred some milk into her coffee.

"Except you." Luke smiled across the table at Ally. "You never doubted him. You two must have a pretty special connection. I'm sure he's going to be grateful for how you stood up for him. Maybe you two will finally get the chance to see where that connection will lead."

"What Brent and I have is history, a whole lot of history." Ally offered a nostalgic smile. "We were kids, who dated a bit and then became good friends. We knew a lot of each other's secrets growing up. I guess, there's something about being young that makes you a little more open and honest."

"Maybe so," Luke agreed.

"But there's nothing romantic between us anymore. He's more like a long lost brother than a long lost love," she said. "I just hope that Connor and Brent's families will be able to put their arguments to rest now."

"Me too." He took the last swallow of his coffee. "Look, I don't want to keep you. I know that you need your rest. There will be endless forms to fill out, but all of that can wait. Take care of yourself, Ally, all right?" He stood up from the table. Ally stood up as well. She forgot about her messy hair, her unwashed face and her ratty robe. All she saw was the man who had saved her life standing before her.

"Luke, thank you." She stared into his eyes. Somehow she was sure that words could never express the amount of gratitude that she actually felt in that moment.

"Anytime Ally." He smiled. Then he shook his head. "Well, hopefully it won't happen again."

Ally laughed. "If it does, I expect a repeat performance."

As Luke started to turn towards the door Ally felt a rush of panic. It wasn't fear that she would be hurt, or fear that Julian would escape. It was fear that she might never get another chance to do what she had been aching to do since they had stood in Julian's driveway.

"Luke wait." Ally rushed forward as he turned back towards her. She opened her arms and embraced him. "Thank you," she whispered. Luke wrapped his arms around her. The moment she felt his embrace every ounce of fear that remained within her disappeared. Luke held her so close that she suspected he felt something similar. It was as if the world stopped spinning for just an instant to give them both the experience of truly connecting. Charlotte pretended to stir her coffee.

"I'm glad you're safe, Ally," Luke murmured beside her ear. "Stay that way, okay?"

Ally smiled as she pulled away from him. "I'll try."

He held her gaze for a moment longer, then he nodded to Charlotte. "You too. Don't think you're getting out of a bit of a discussion about when to call the police. Hmm?"

Charlotte raised her coffee to him. "Anything you say, Detective." She offered an innocent smile. Ally knew that smile meant more trouble than Luke could ever dream of handling. Luke looked between the two and shook his head. Then he turned and stepped out the door. Ally stared after him.

"What was that all about?" Charlotte spoke in a sing-song tone.

"I'm just grateful," Ally muttered. She avoided looking directly at her grandmother.

"Uh huh, that's a whole lot of gratitude I just witnessed." Charlotte giggled behind her mug of coffee.

"Mee-Maw!" Ally shook her head as she sat back down at the table. "He saved my life. How do you even say thank you for something like that?"

"You can't really. But I think he might have saved more than that." Charlotte offered a wise wink.

"I don't know about that," Ally lied through her teeth. She knew just what her grandmother meant. For the first time since her divorce Ally didn't have that subtle ache in the core of her heart. It was simply gone. It was replaced with a curiosity, a wonder about the future, and whether Luke might just be part of it.

"Mee-Maw is always right, remember that." Charlotte sipped her coffee. "I hope you plan on staying a bit longer to recover. Traveling in your condition would not be a good idea. Then there's getting the shop straightened out," Charlotte continued to ramble on about all of the reasons that Ally should stay.

"Actually." Ally looked across the table at her grandmother. "I was hoping to stay longer than that. What do you think, Mee-Maw?" Ally's heart skipped a beat. She knew it was what she wanted, but it was still hard to think about such a huge change.

"Yes!" Charlotte laughed out loud and jumped up from the table. "Yes, that's what I think!"

"I'll help you run the shop," Ally offered. She was excited by her grandmother's joy.

"And I could finally move into the retirement village!" Charlotte's eyes glowed with excitement.

"You don't have to do that, Mee-Maw." Ally shook her head. "I can get my own place. You've lived in this cottage for a long time, it's your home."

"You'll do no such thing. This cottage belongs to the women of our family. I've had it long enough. Now it will be yours. I'm ready for a little pampering, and to be around my friends. Besides we'll still see each other every day at the shop. Right?"

"Right." Ally nodded. She smiled at her grandmother.

"The only thing is you'll probably have to keep Arnold here." Charlotte smiled. "I don't think they will let me bring him with."

"Of course." Ally nodded. "Arnold is a part of the cottage. I couldn't imagine him living anywhere else."

"I'll come walk him every day." Ally felt content at the thought of seeing her grandmother every day.

After all that she had been through, returning to the city seemed like the strange thing to do. Calling Blue River home again felt like the right thing to do. She loved the people, even with their flaws. She loved the memories she had of her mother, and of growing up in the little town. Most of all she realized she'd rather spend her time with the wisest woman that she knew than all of the culture the city offered. Charlotte still had a lot to teach her and Ally was looking forward to learning it.

Maybe, somewhere in the middle of all of that she would have the opportunity to really get to know Luke. He had enough to deal with being new to town and now the only detective in Blue River. She was sure that he could use a friendly face around town. Now Ally only had to break the news to Peaches that she was going to be Arnold's permanent housemate. She giggled at the thought. Ally never expected that her visit home would turn into a permanent move, but nothing had ever felt more right to her.

The End

Triple Chocolate Muffin Recipe

Ingredients:

3 ounces butter

6 ounces semisweet chocolate

3 cups all-purpose flour

1 tablespoon baking powder

3 tablespoons unsweetened cocoa powder

1 cup light brown sugar

2 teaspoons vanilla extract

1 1/2 cups milk

2 eggs

4 ounces milk chocolate cut into chunks

3 ounces white chocolate cut into chunks

Preparation:

Preheat oven to 350 degrees Fahrenheit.

Line a 12 hole muffin tin with paper liners.

Melt butter and semisweet chocolate.

Sift flour, baking powder and cocoa into a bowl. Add light brown sugar and mix the dry ingredients together.

In another bowl whisk vanilla extract, milk and eggs together. Add to the dry ingredients and fold until combined.

Mix in lukewarm melted chocolate and butter mixture.

Mix in white and milk chocolate chunks. Leaving some small pieces to decorate the top of the muffins.

Spoon mixture into muffin cups.

Sprinkle leftover chocolate chunks on the top of the batter.

Bake in the preheated oven for 18 minutes or until a skewer inserted into the middle of the muffins comes out clean.

Cool on a wire rack.

More Cozy Mysteries by Cindy Bell

Sage Gardens Cozy Mysteries

Birthdays Can Be Deadly

Money Can Be Deadly

Trust Can Be Deadly

Dune House Cozy Mysteries

Seaside Secrets

Boats and Bad Guys

Treasured History

Hidden Hideaways

Dodgy Dealings

Suspects and Surprises

Wendy the Wedding Planner Cozy Mysteries

Matrimony, Money and Murder

Chefs, Ceremonies and Crimes

Knives and Nuptials

Mice, Marriage and Murder

Heavenly Highland Inn Cozy Mysteries

Murdering the Roses

Dead in the Daisies

Killing the Carnations

Drowning the Daffodils

Suffocating the Sunflowers

Books, Bullets and Blooms

A Deadly serious Gardening Contest

A Bridal Bouquet and a Body

Bekki the Beautician Cozy Mysteries

Hairspray and Homicide

A Dyed Blonde and a Dead Body

Mascara and Murder

Pageant and Poison

Conditioner and a Corpse

Mistletoe, Makeup and Murder

Hairpin, Hair Dryer and Homicide

Blush, a Bride and a Body

Shampoo and a Stiff

Cosmetics, a Cruise and a Killer

Lipstick, a Long Iron and Lifeless

Camping, Concealer and Criminals

Treated and Dyed

Made in the USA
Coppell, TX
27 November 2022